He That Has an Ear, Let Him Hear

Armillary Series

De Von Bell and Tiffany Duvernay

He That Has an Ear, Let Him Hear
Armillary Series

Copyright © 2008 by Quantum Door Publishing, Inc. All rights reserved.

Armillary Series concept: De Von Bell
Page layout and design: De Von Bell
Cover design: Tiffany Duvernay
Editing: Karen Driscoll, Tiffany Duvernay

Discounts are available for bulk purchases for seminars, sales promotions, premiums, fund-raising, educational or institutional use. E-mail us sales@qdexperience.com.

Universities or seminary schools interested in the QD Experience and QD articles and media (e-books, audio-books, and videos) should email seminars@qdexperience.com.

www.qdexperience.com
www.quantumdoorpub.com

ISBN 978-0-6152-2188-5

He that has an Ear,

Let him hear

By **De Von Bell**

Technical Research by
De Von Bell
Tiffany Duvernay

Quantum Door Publishing © 2008

Contents

WWW.QDEXPERIENCE.COM

INTRODUCTION

He That Has an Ear, Let Him Hear is a documentation of a movement that has been in existence for over 2000 years. It is a movement that many have called Christianity. Christianity has been viewed as a practice that is studied and followed by those who receive the teachings of the proclaimed Son of God. People have considered the leader of this movement to be the one and only begotten son of the living God. I too have worshiped the person called Jesus since I was a very little boy. I was told that Christ died on the cross for my sins and for the sins of the world, which I took great comfort. Many people have been told that Christ is the English term for the Greek word (*Christós*), which literally means "*The Anointed One.*" The Hebrew word for Christ is (*Masíah*, usually transliterated *Messiah*). But is the translation accurate? We'll find out.

It is true that the word may be misunderstood by some as being the surname of Jesus due to the frequent juxtaposition of *Jesus* and *Christ* in the Christian Bible as well as other Christian writings. Often used as a more formal-sounding synonym for Jesus, the word "Christ" is in fact a title, hence its common reciprocal use *Christ Jesus,* meaning *The Anointed One, Jesus.*

But the word "Christ" did not originate as the name for the anointed one, at least not for the Jesus that I was told about. Christ is a name that is more synonymous with the anointing of a different person in history who relates to Egypt and who will be discussed in a later chapter.

You see, many Christians profess their love for Christ, and their allegiance to Christ. Many have said the Lord's Prayer and accepted Christ as their Lord and Savior. I did the same back when I was 6 years old and I've rededicated my life many times over to Christ, continually. Now I worship the true living God and the true Son of God, but I call him the Messiah, not the Christ. I pray to Yahushúa, which some say is Hebrew for Jesus, continually. I was relieved to know that I was dealing with semantics. Or was I?

5

But that's what happens when you are dealing with the passion for the word of God. I would and still do get very excited about reading the word of God and researching what the words mean, what the origins of the words are, if the word came from the Greek or the Hebrew. Do I need to go study Greek or Hebrew? I mean, hey, I'm down for that. I love reading the Bible. I want more, teach me more. That's what I say to my surroundings.

How much do you love the word of God? Do you bury yourself into the Bible continually? So do I, the King James Version that is. Hey, do you have some time on your hands? I would love to share with you some of the things that I found out while reading the Bible and while looking up their meanings. You know I get so giddy about the word of God that, well, I just want to know it all. I want to know the truth.

Do you want to know the truth? Are you willing to research and work with me on finding the truth? GREAT!!! We can start immediately.

OK, grab this book, your Bible, a couple of encyclopedias, some coffee, a pen and lots of paper. Oh, wait a minute, do you have access to the internet? This is even better, since the Bible and encyclopedia are online these days.

OK, grab a computer, a highlighter, your Bible, and let's do it. This is great.

Oh, wait; before we start I must inform you that there are ground rules. We are searching for the truth. Many people don't do this kind of extensive studying, but I'll do most of the work. I need for you to check the work and see if what I dig up is true or not. We'll be a team. Hey, this is great. I'm excited.

Oh, one other thing, and this is important: our research is between you and me. We need to read these things for ourselves. Don't be lazy! People don't take time to find out the truth, they always want someone to tell them what the truth is. If you want to, ask your pastor or who some say are the leading authorities on Christianity. He or she might not have done their research. Hey, it happens. Just because someone is a minister, does not mean they know every answer. The best that they can do is tell you they heard an answer from someone else and that answer in many cases doesn't apply to the question. Not enough people read things for themselves. Keep in mind that the leading authority of theology would most likely give you opinions on things that lead to dead ends. Like if you ask where Cain's wife came from, you will be told Eve had twins, two boys and two girls. But wait; there is no record of that. If you ask where that is written, they will likely say, "Oh women weren't documented in the scriptures in those days, where they came from is not important, just believe or ask God when you get to Heaven." Well as far as you and I are concerned, we are searching for the truth, and not someone's opinion.

Come go with me on a journey for the truth. Let's learn some things together. Let's give the reading of the word one big encore.

LET HIM HEAR

CHAPTER 1

In Christianity, there is a discipline that many believers and unbelievers follow. It is called the Holy Bible, the King James Version to be exact. In many countries, including the United States, laws are written with morals and conduct paralleling this book. It is actually a compilation of 66 books bound together and called as one (The King James Version of the Bible).

"He that has ears to hear, let him hear." Mark 4th chapter 9th verse.

This is a statement chanted by the authors of the books of Mark, Matthew, Luke, John, Acts and even Revelation. It is a statement that the Messiah is stating over and over again, yet many scholars and ministers of these same books find themselves glossing over and dismissing it as a method used by the Messiah to polarize his audience into considering special attention to what he had to say as if it was and still is irrelevant to the content that would preside before and after. But was it? Is it? Surely the text is arguably written by ghost writers. Some scholars and ministers have resolved within their minds that such writings were directly from the apostles themselves and named after the men who wrote such accounts. Let's examine the phrase in question. The writers of these books made sure the reader of such statements would also find a juncture within one's mind to either draw nearer to what was being disseminated, or continue to listen to what was being said while observing the content in the third person. Was it a coded message sent to what the Messiah called the Lost Sheep of Israel?

Arguably, many have stated that the Messiah has come for the salvation of the entire world. But what did the Messiah state? Did he say he came for the whole entire world? I ask you: What does the whole entire world consist of? Do you know? Have you even considered what the world consists of? Moses states this about the world, Paul says that about the world, but what does the Messiah state?

> For God so loved the world, that he gave his only begotten Son, that whosoever believeth in him should not perish, but have everlasting life. (John 3:16)

People use this verse as a qualifier for why they find themselves justified in recruiting any and everybody they come across, inviting them to become members of the family of God (Christianity). Yet, it's important to identify when the Lord says the world what is actually being said.

If you found yourself in a court of law, as would a lawyer, the legal counsel would find themselves arguing legal statutes and interpretations of case law as it relates to what's established in those statutes and also what has been adjudicated by certain judges. In doing so, the same counsel would search feverishly for things that qualify and disqualify certain statutes and case law. In like manner, according to the Bible, a true believer should study the word of God to rightly divide the word of truth. If a qualifier or disqualifier presents itself you must accompany the initial thought with the trailing qualifier or disqualifier.

In Matthew 15:22-28 the Messiah was inquired by a Canaanite woman if he could heal her daughter. The Messiah stated in the 24th verse, "I am sent only to the Lost Sheep of Israel". The woman pleaded, "Help me." Then the Messiah replied, "It is not right to take the children's bread and toss it to dogs." Here, I'll let you read it for yourself:

> And, behold, a woman of Canaan came out of the same coasts, and cried

unto him, saying, Have mercy on me, O Lord, thou son of David; my daughter is grievously vexed with a devil.

But he answered her not a word. And his disciples came and besought him, saying, Send her away; for she crieth after us.

But he answered and said, **I am not sent but unto the lost sheep of the house of Israel.**

Then came she and worshipped him, saying, Lord, help me.

But he answered and said, **It is not meet to take the children's bread, and to cast it to dogs.**

And she said, Truth, Lord: yet the dogs eat of the crumbs which fall from their masters' table.

Then Jesus answered and said unto her, **O woman, great is thy faith: be it unto thee even as thou wilt.** And her daughter was made whole from that very hour. (Matthew

15:22-28)

I ask: does this dialogue disqualify the statements in John 3:16? Is the Messiah here for the whole world or is he here for the Lost Sheep of Israel? Are you a believer? Well if so, then you will arguably take both statements as true. Similar to the laws of the land, one statement can stand in its own righteousness foregoing a disqualifier that filters the embodied content. The books of the Bible display many qualifiers and disqualifiers throughout, but for the sake of argument let's treat such text like a deck of cards. If the Messiah states it, then his statements trump those statements of prophets and apostles. Though their writings are inspired, many statements are opinionated and wisely stated to be such by the author. To thoroughly examine the content of these books, let's reference and match information from the many books to what is written in "red letter", or shall I say the accounted statements of The Messiah.

In the book of Revelation there is a record of war that took place. Revelation 12:7-12 states:

And there was war in heaven: Michael and his angels fought against the dragon; and the dragon fought and his angels,

And prevailed not; neither was their place found any more in heaven.

And the great dragon was cast out, that old serpent, called the Devil, and Satan, which deceiveth the whole world: he was cast out into the earth, and his angels were cast out with him.

And I heard a loud voice saying in heaven, Now is come salvation, and strength, and the kingdom of our God, and the power of his Christ: for the accuser of our brethren is cast down, which accused them before our God day and night.

*And they overcame him by the blood of
the Lamb, and by the word of their
testimony; and they loved not their lives
unto the death.*

*Therefore rejoice, [ye] heavens, and ye
that dwell in them. Woe to the
inhabiters of the earth and of the sea!
for the devil is come down unto you,
having great wrath, because he
knoweth that he hath but a short time.
(Matthew 12:7-12)*

Where did they go after they were cast down? Did Satan continue
to walk the earth as a spirit, taking no mortal form, or even an animal
form? Were he and his angels' just puffs of smoke or are they among
us? What if they are among us and look just like us, talking the talk,
yet knowing their fate and hating the Messiah and the Lost Sheep he
has Sheppard along with those he has herded together? What if the
Messiah, knowing that he was walking among the shadows of death
and fearing no evil, being himself as it may, communicated unto his
sheep as if they alone would know his voice and they alone would
hear it and become converted with passion and intrigued to
commune with such a divine soul (the Messiah that is) as they are
drawn to him with uncontrollable passion.

John 10:7 My sheep hear my voice, and
I know them, and they follow me:

We have found ourselves chanting that the chosen people, or
should I say the people of God, are the Israelis or the Jews. In the
many writings of Paul to the different churches he states comments
to the Jews first and then to the Gentiles. But I share with you on this
day that based on my research the chosen people are not based
on biological DNA or should we say by birth, but Spiritual DNA.

Well, the Messiah talked in parables continually to audibly
disseminate his thoughts unto the Lost Sheep without exposing his
true statements to the evil ones. His sheep, being of Spiritual DNA,
would hear his voice and be compelled while those who did not
were as such because they were not of him, nor were they ordained
to ever be of him from the beginning of time. His time here was not

only to reconcile the true children of God into the Kingdom through his death, but to bring about additional awakenings within the Lost Sheep through his communications and the writings of the scriptures and other books for those of us today. For example, Matthew 7:13-15 states:

> *Enter ye in at the strait gate: for wide [is] the gate, and broad [is] the way, that leadeth to destruction, and many there be which go in thereat:*
>
> *Because strait [is] the gate, and narrow [is] the way, which leadeth unto life, and few there be that find it.*
>
> *Beware of false prophets, which come to you in sheep's clothing, but inwardly they are ravening wolves.*

According to Matthew 7:13-14, the Messiah is identifying parameters and markers to look for in life as one of his Lost Sheep. He continues to find himself warning his sheep, his children, by keeping them in a state of awareness: If you see this, know that it means that. If you see that, then know that it means this; similar to an "oracle" in a video game helping the characters to get through the game and hopefully avoiding pitfalls. It continues...

> *Ye shall know them by their fruits. Do men gather grapes of thorns, or figs of thistles?*
>
> *Even so every good tree bringeth forth good fruit; but a corrupt tree bringeth forth evil fruit.*
>
> *A good tree cannot bring forth evil fruit, neither [can] a corrupt tree bring forth good fruit.* (Matthew 7:16-18)

The Messiah continues to admonish his sheep with measurements of clarity by making unshakable, inconvertible statements about Spiritual DNA. "The tree that is good brings forth good fruit and cannot bring forth bad fruit" is not what you hear in church nowadays. The church messages have become seminars on how to evolve from a bad person to a good person. Have you noticed how ministers find themselves preaching and teaching from the writings of Paul? Constantly telling their flock how to be a good Christian and that they must keep trying, all the while instilling practically unreachable levels of transformation. You have individuals in the church nowadays who are thoroughly frustrated with why they can't stop sinning and when they get to church they hear the same message, "You've got to love somebody" or is it "everybody"? Come on minister, We want the truth. Tell me why this world is so evil. Don't you want to say that? If we are at war, then tell me the truth so that I may defend myself. Not "You've got to love everybody." It continues...

Every tree that bringeth not forth good fruit is hewn down, and cast into the fire.

Wherefore by their fruits ye shall know them. (Matthew 7:19-20)

If you want to know who is of the evil one versus who is of the Lord, you will know them by their fruits. Watch how they carry themselves. Now really, how many memberships can you sell if your potential members are told, "We may not change you, but we'll give you a litmus test to determine whether you are one of us or not."
Later in that same chapter, the author stated in the 28th and 29th verses:

And it came to pass, when Jesus had ended these sayings, the people were astonished at his doctrine:

For he taught them as [one] having authority, and not as the scribes. (Matthew 7:28-29)

14

According to my research, many in church today are of the evil one. Some are even the children of the light and darkness who married and, through birth of their children possess, both measurements of the chosen and the evil one within their Spiritual DNA due to the fact that flesh begets flesh and spirit begets spirit. Both are merged and become one. I'll elaborate:

According to Matthew 13 more than one type of human is walking this earth: (a) a child of the light is ordained from the beginning of time containing Spiritual DNA, fully capable of receiving the word of God, who carry themselves accordingly, (b) those individuals who are rotten to the core, who look like us, talk like us, are not human, but carry the likeness of human flesh, and (c) cross breeds who are the product of man, who find themselves excepting their fate similar to an embryo excepting its gender. A cross breed is the type of individual that you would most likely find walking this earth. It gets cloudy for believers when it comes to being able to discern the company they keep. While observing an inconsistency in the character of surrounding individuals, most observers give the benefit of the doubt and reach out to influence those surrounding them to conduct themselves in the manner that the Messiah, Paul and others have stated. Again, like an embryo accepting its gender, the cross breed would lean toward one side of the spectrum or the other, regardless of the campaigns given by accompanying individuals who continue to reproof their companions with possible improvements or motivation such as repent and you can change.

Just as there is more than one type of human, we are more likely to accept the fact that there is more than one type of spirit: good spirits and bad spirits. Esoterically you have Angels (Gatekeepers) and Demons from the Evil one.

Let us look at the moment of impact when a cross breed is becoming born again and shedding their alter ego. It's the moment when the embryo chooses its gender, a ritual that has quantum physical application. The cross breed who is a child of the light internally, not mentally, accepts his or her fate as a person who possesses both Spiritual DNA's and desires to eliminate the Spiritual DNA of the evil one by excepting the Messiah as Lord over their life and not lord themselves into hell. Based on your DNA makeup, you can't bare the fruit of a good tree until the bad is eliminated. Your fruit will taste bitter sweet.

Nicodemus, a cross breed who was a Pharisee, went to the Messiah to ask him about such phenomenal awakenings that were taking place among the people. By his acknowledging that he'd been contemplating the Kingdom of God, Jesus answered him in a method similar to how he'd answered Peter in the book of Matthew when he stated that only the spirit of God could have told such things to Peter. This confirmed Nicodemus' ability to see the Kingdom, which was not for the average man to see, but because Nicodemus was of the Lost Sheep, even as a Pharisee he was able to see the Kingdom. Let's read John 3:1-7:

There was a man of the Pharisees, named Nicodemus, a ruler of the Jews:

The same came to Jesus by night, and said unto him, Rabbi, we know that thou art a teacher come from God: for no man can do these miracles that thou doest, except God be with him.

Jesus answered and said unto him, **Verily, verily, I say unto thee, Except a man be born again, he cannot see the kingdom of God.**
Nicodemus saith unto him, How can a man be born when he is old? can he enter the second time into his mother's womb, and be born?

Jesus answered, **Verily, verily, I say unto thee, Except a man be born of water and [of] the Spirit, he cannot enter into the kingdom of God.**

That which is born of the flesh is flesh; and that which is born of the Spirit is spirit.

Marvel not that I said unto thee, Ye must be born again. *(John 3:1-7)*

16

Now as you can see and according to the Bible the Messiah continues to make a difference between those that can see and hear what's really being said and the significance of being able.

Hey are all Jews or Israelis considered to be "the chosen"? Well let's ask the Messiah for who had a very interesting conversation with a group of Jews. Mind you, the question is, "Are all Jews considered chosen"? Remember the trump card called the Messiah in that deck of cards? Well, the Messiah card trumps all opinions and serves as a qualifier or disqualifier of the content written in the many books of the King James Version of the Bible.

In the next writings, the Messiah is clearly testifying to a group of Jews about the authenticity of them not being heirs to the Kingdom by proxy of physical DNA. Yet he stresses that it is the Spiritual DNA that determines being of the chosen ones. The Messiah begins by qualifying who he is by what authority he speaks, and based on Spiritual DNA, some in the crowd immediately believed him and others did not. Check out these writings in John 8th chapter beginning in verse 26:

> *I have many things to say and to judge of you: but he that sent me is true; and I speak to the world those things which I have heard of him.*
>
> *They understood not that he spake to them of the Father.*
>
> *Then said Jesus unto them, When ye have lifted up the Son of man, then shall ye know that I am [he], and [that] I do nothing of myself; but as my Father hath taught me, I speak these things.*
>
> *And he that sent me is with me: the Father hath not left me alone; for I do always those things that please him.*

> *As he spake these words, many believed*
> *on him. (John 8:26-30)*

Next, he shares with the group of Jews that belong to the Lost Sheep, that if they continue in his teachings then they are his disciples indeed. He alludes to the fact that by doing so the truth will be revealed to them and the truth will set them free from the ones who are unaware of such accounts and free them from the entrapments of being in the dark.

> *Then said Jesus to those Jews which*
> *believed on him,* **If ye continue in my**
> **word, [then] are ye my disciples indeed;**
>
> **And ye shall know the truth, and the truth**
> **shall make you free.** *(John 8:31-32)*

The other Jews who were unable to hear or see inquired of the Messiah.

> *They answered him, We be Abraham's*
> *seed, and were never in bondage to any*
> *man: how sayest thou, Ye shall be made*
> *free?*
>
> *Jesus answered them,* **Verily, verily, I say**
> **unto you, Whosoever committeth sin is the**
> **servant of sin.**
>
> **And the servant abideth not in the house**
> **for ever: [but] the Son**
> **abideth ever.** *(John 8:33-35)*

Whoever abides with sin shall not abide in the house of the Lord and is not eligible for the life style of the house. The Messiah however, without sin, abides within the house of the Lord forever.

> **If the Son therefore shall make you free,**
> **ye shall be free indeed.** *(verse 36)*

All who assume that all Jews are the chosen ones need to pay close attention to the next writings in John:

> *I know that ye are Abraham's seed; but*
> *ye seek to kill me, because my word hath*
> *no place in you.*
>
> *I speak that which I have seen with my*
> *Father: and ye do that which ye have*
> *seen with your father.*
>
> They answered and said unto him,
> Abraham is our father. Jesus saith unto
> them, **If ye were Abraham's children, ye**
> **would do the works of Abraham.**
>
> **But now ye seek to kill me, a man that**
> **hath told you the truth, which I have**
> **heard of God: this did not Abraham.**
>
> **Ye do the deeds of your father.** Then said
> they to him, We be not born of
> fornication; we have one Father, [even]
> God. (John 8:37-41)

In verses 8:42-59 Jesus mocks the evil ones, taunting them about their inability to understand him while others in the same crowd could. He points out that their true nature and Spiritual DNA are evil.

> **Jesus said unto them, If God were your**
> **Father, ye would love me: for I proceeded**
> **forth and came from God; neither came I**
> **of myself, but he sent me.**
>
> **Why do ye not understand my speech?**
> **[even] because ye cannot hear my word.**
>
> **Ye are of [your] father the devil, and the**
> **lusts of your father ye will do. He was a**
> **murderer from the beginning, and abode**
> **not in the truth, because there is no truth**

in him. When he speaketh a lie, he speaketh of his own: for he is a liar, and the father of it.

And because I tell [you] the truth, ye believe me not.

Which of you convinceth me of sin? And if I say the truth, why do ye not believe me?

He that is of God heareth God's words: ye therefore hear [them] not, because ye are not of God.

Then answered the Jews, and said unto him, Say we not well that thou art a Samaritan, and hast a devil?

Jesus answered, I have not a devil; but I honour my Father, and ye do dishonour me.

And I seek not mine own glory: there is one that seeketh and judgeth.

Verily, verily, I say unto you, If a man keep my saying, he shall never see death.

Then said the Jews unto him, Now we know that thou hast a devil. Abraham is dead, and the prophets; and thou sayest, If a man keep my saying, he shall never taste of death.

Art thou greater than our father Abraham, which is dead? and the prophets are dead: whom makest thou thyself?

Jesus answered, If I honour myself, my honour is nothing: it is my Father that

*honoureth me; of whom ye say, that he is
your God:*

*Yet ye have not known him; but I know
him: and if I should say, I know him not, I
shall be a liar like unto you: but I know
him, and keep his saying.*

*Your father Abraham rejoiced to see my
day: and he saw [it], and was glad.*

*Then said the Jews unto him, Thou art not
yet fifty years old, and hast thou seen
Abraham?*

Jesus said unto them, **Verily, verily, I say
unto you, Before Abraham was, I am.**

*Then took they up stones to cast at him:
but Jesus hid himself, and went out of the
temple, going through the midst of them,
and so passed by
(John 8:42-59).*

Many ministers and scholars share the separatist viewpoint that you
have Jews and Gentiles only. **Wrong!** The rest of the world exists.
Genesis chapter 10 mentions the "isles of the Gentiles", but there
were more people were on this earth than only those descendants
of Israel and of the islands of the Gentiles (Asia Minor), which was
lower Europe near and upon Greece. In that day, the world was
comprised of Egypt, the rest of Africa, Asia, and the rest of the
Roman Empire.

Now initially Paul's ministry was geared toward the lower European
nations as well as the Jews and when establishing his writing to many
of the different churches, which later became the books of the New
Testament, he continued to make distinctions between the two. In
that day people struggled with the radical views of Paul who invited
non-Jews to hear teachings and receive according to their belief.
Now remember there were Paul's teachings, and then there were
the teachings of the Messiah. If one said "white" and other said
"black" as they referenced the same observations, but relayed

different interpretations of what was being requested, which one would you accept: the Messiah or Paul?

While the Messiah was alive he told his disciples not to go and proclaim the gospel to the Gentiles while Paul said that after the Messiah's death he was approached on the road to Damascus by the Messiah who commissioned him to spread the word of the Gospel to the Gentiles. Well here, I'll let you read it:

> These twelve Jesus sent forth, and commanded them, saying, **Go not into the way of the Gentiles, and into [any] city of the Samaritans enter ye not:**
>
> **But go rather to the lost sheep of the house of Israel.**
>
> **And as ye go, preach, saying, The kingdom of heaven is at hand.** (Matthew 10:5-7)

Now According to Acts 9:15 Ananias was sent by God to approach Saul, soon to become Paul, and tell him that he will be used as a vessel to carry the gospel to the Gentiles. Well here, I'll let you read it:

> But the Lord said unto him, Go thy way: for he is a chosen vessel unto me, to bear my name before the Gentiles, and kings, and the children of Israel: (Acts 9:15)

Now it's obvious in retrospect to look at what the Lord established in the making of history and what events would bring us to today-- predestination that is. But the Messiah states, "proclaim the gospel to the Lost Sheep of Israel and not to the Gentiles". Oh I guess you would say historical reference doesn't count and you have to believe that both testimonies are accurate and true.

Did I say believe? I would be doing you a great injustice if I did not talk on belief before going further.

According to the Bible, being a true believer is not based on whether someone says Lord, Lord, but by the conduct of their character. Energy flows from within and then broadcasts outwardly. How they carry themselves to the end is very important--how they carry themselves to the end.

"Once saved, always saved." Not! Once you have crossed over the great divide between this life and the next is the time you will know if you are saved. Until then, faithfully seek the truth and don't let anyone deceive you into a false sense of complacency and self-righteousness...at least that was what I was taught, but...

Most organizations or modern day churches would refute what's being stated in our study, but remember what I've said; they are more interested in membership than enlightenment. Study to show yourself approved. Also, what's written in red letter trumps the opinions of other writing in the Bible.

We are told that what are written in red letter are direct statements from the Messiah. There is a distinct difference between a direct statement and an inspired statement, similar to a true documentary and a movie inspired by true events. Direct statements are made on face value. An inspired statement requires the ability for the author to explain his experience or the accountings to the best of his ability, such as some of the writings of Paul. You see Paul was putting together the organization called the church, rivaling many established religions and worships at that time. He was propositioned with many questions that the Messiah may not have spoken on, or at least they were not documented. When such an event arose, he qualified his statements by saying, "As for me", or "I, not the Lord" is saying this, whether it was to the church of Corinth, Romans, Ephesus, or whomever.

Remember we are studying here. Why do you look like that? Hey, I feel passionate about the writings of Paul, but we must keep them in their proper content. He was structuring the policies and procedures of this new religion (People of The Way). He was writing letters to the churches or you can call them the new communities, mostly in response to questions that were sent to him from congregations being that he'd had a personal encounter with the Messiah.

Am I saying that Paul's writings do not matter? No, they do, but if you are in conflict with Paul's opinions and what is written according to the gospels: the books of Matthew, Mark, Luke and John, along with the book of Acts, then use qualifiers to filter the information for its accuracy. Red letter trumps all. Remember the trump card called the Messiah in that deck of cards? Then let's be consistent and agree that red letter trumps all being that they are defined as the very words of the Messiah.

Let's cover something spoken of earlier. Are there others that walk the earth? Well let's read Matthew, 13th chapter. Jesus was talking to a multitude of people consisting of the Lost Sheep and the evil ones. He shares a series of parables back to back referencing the same subject, expounding on the Kingdom of God and sharing things about the inhibitors on this earth that have been hidden since the beginning of time. Notice how he breaks things down plainly to his disciples later, after the crowd leaves, so plain that it does not need any interpretation and yet many seminary schools warn against young ministers preaching from this text because it is so explosive that it will blow the doors off of those very same seminary school's true motives for teaching individuals on how to teach the Bible; should I say it would be bad for business? Oh, you did not know. Hmmmm....

The mission of the majority of churches today is the business of recruiting men and women into the club called "the church" while promising them salvation based on so many things that are unscriptural. The true leaders of the church don't want you to know the truth; only what they say is the truth in order to control the masses. Don't question them or they'll say you don't believe.

One of the most direct statements from the Messiah that justifies the understanding of the Lost Sheep versus the evil ones is Matthew 13:24-51. I'll let you read a good portion of the chapter for yourself. In it you will find The Messiah talking to the Lost Sheep through a series of parables, one after the other, luring the Lost Sheep into a measurement of clarity by defining more details in the following parables than in the previous one. Well I'll let you read before I continue:

> Another parable put he forth unto them, saying, **The kingdom of heaven is likened unto a man which sowed good seed in his field:**

24

But while men slept, his enemy came and sowed tares among the wheat, and went his way.

But when the blade was sprung up, and brought forth fruit, then appeared the tares also.

So the servants of the householder came and said unto him, Sir, didst not thou sow good seed in thy field? from whence then hath it tares?

He said unto them, An enemy hath done this. The servants said unto him, Wilt thou then that we go and gather them up?

But he said, Nay; lest while ye gather up the tares, ye root up also the wheat with them.

Let both grow together until the harvest: and in the time of harvest I will say to the reapers, Gather ye together first the tares, and bind them in bundles to burn them: but gather the wheat into my barn. *(Matthew 13:24-30)*

Amazing how you can ask 13 different ministers what this means and there would be a good chance that they will not give you the same answer. Maybe one of them would direct you to the verses below where you can hear what the Messiah meant from his own mouth. He continues:

All these things spake Jesus unto the multitude in parables; and without a parable spake he not unto them:

That it might be fulfilled which was spoken by the prophet, saying, I will open my mouth in parables; I will utter

things which have been kept secret
from the foundation of the world.
(Matthew 13:34-35)

He will utter things which have been kept secret from the beginning
of the world. When I was a kid they did not tell me that Jesus kept
secrets. They said Christ loves you, and he'll do anything you ask if
you ask him. Not! At least not the way I was taught. Good thing I
grew up to learn the love of the Messiah for myself and the reality of
what's really going on. Or did I? I know he loves me, I understand
with more clarity on asking something in his name now. Thank you
Lord! Let's see how the Messiah defined the parable:

Then Jesus sent the multitude away, and
went into the house: and his disciples
came unto him, saying, Declare unto us
the parable of the tares of the field.

He answered and said unto them, He that
soweth the good seed is the Son of man;

The field is the world; the good seed are
the children of the kingdom; but the tares
are the children of the wicked one;

The enemy that sowed them is the devil;
the harvest is the end of the world; and
the reapers are the angels.

As therefore the tares are gathered and
burned in the fire; so shall it be in the end
of this world.

The Son of man shall send forth his angels,
and they shall gather out of his kingdom
all things that offend, and them which do
iniquity;

And shall cast them into a furnace of fire:
there shall be wailing and gnashing of
teeth.

Then shall the righteous shine forth as the sun in the kingdom of their Father. Who hath ears to hear, let him hear. (Matthew 13:36-43)

Again, the Messiah is suggesting to those who have ears to hear, "Let him hear", and mind you he is among his disciples now. The crowd is gone. Most Christians are fed goody, goody, information and words of continual encouragement, but if they are not being fed these things some may accuse the speaker of being cynical or hating the church. I'm not here to speak words of continual encouragement and I don't hate the church. I dislike the evil ones that are controlling the church and starving the masses with messages that leave the church with no power. Couldn't the earlier church have taken a different view on good vs. evil than that of the church today? I think so.

Did you see where he stated that the devil has planted his children on earth? Can you handle that, or will your mind just overlook what you just read? People are so focused on maintaining a false impression of their preferred status with God, which is demonstrated when their feelings get in the way of what the Bible states. You see them flip-flopping from good to evil constantly throughout the day as if at 8:00am in morning we are God's children, but by 12:30pm we act up and now we belong to Satan, or how does Flip Wilson say it? "The Devil made me do it!" Then by 3:00pm that same day we belong to God again. Stop it people. It is not about attitudes or feelings. "I feel holy. I feel naughty." It's about what is in you. What you truly are. Earlier we discussed looking at the fruits. Later I will be touching on Paul's writings to the Gentiles and Jews' regarding relationships between the earlier church and the Jewish Pharisees, the proper interpretation of the letters that became the books of Romans, Corinthians, Ephesians, and so on. It is imperative that we come to read the Bible accurately and ask the following questions: (a) Who is the author? (b) Who was the audience at the time? c) What is the time dispensation? Etc.

There are so many misinterpretations of the writings in the Bible that many live in darkness. I have heard it preached by prosperity preachers that the covenants were for all men who believed. Now, were the covenants to specific people at the time they were made, or to the entire world?

Have you heard the poetry of the Psalm of David (which was personal worship between David and God) blasted through the church as if they were all inclusive statements of fact geared to all believers? The relationship that God had with David was what he had with David. Many people today believe and have faith in things based on a lie, thinking something is coming to them because it came to David and standing on it, standing on the lie. Here is the thing: there are some scriptures that are all inclusive, but not the majority. You can not show someone in the Bible that God gave Jimmy a Cadillac Escalade, and he wants to give you one also. No! Stop it. Stop trading potential lottery blessing tickets for tithes.

I have heard many ministers say that Jesus spoke in parables to teach a lesson to people by making up stories and sharing them among the masses to help them understand what is right. Wow! The last time I made up a story I was called a liar. Wrong! Wrong! I don't think that the Messiah is a liar. See that's the trick. If you are God incarnate and cannot lie, then in being omnipotent you may be privileged to some information that others are not. So when he says, there was a man who had three sons, I think he's telling the truth. People, read it for yourselves in the book of Matthew, 13th chapter, verses 10 through 11. What did the Messiah tell his disciples? Come on people this has got to stop. Read it for yourself:

> And the disciples came, and said unto him, Why speakest thou unto them in parables?
>
> He answered and said unto them, **Because it is given unto you to know the mysteries of the kingdom of heaven, but to them it is not given.** (Matthew 13:10-11)

But to them it is not given. Can you say evil ones?

Do you know how many ministers would fight me tooth and nail to keep this kind of awareness from you by saying things like, "Brother, you are trying to get too deep. All we need to know is you got to love everybody." Read the Bible people. Listen to the urgency in the Messiah's voice.

I assure you that this study we are doing will change your life and the way that you will look at what is holy. There is a consorted effort by the evil ones to continue to change the writings and the meanings of the Bible to continue to mislead the masses. The chapters in this book will expound upon significant dialogue. You will learn about the Bible. And for you that are the Lost Sheep...Awaken! Read information for yourselves.

Did you like this study? Good. I like it, and think it is important. Hey you're not offended, are you? Good, because it's about reading and understanding the truth.

Am I therefore become your enemy, because I tell you the truth?
Galatians 4:16

What was that? Oh, the evil ones? Yeah, I had to take a double take on that one myself, but I did my research. Would you like to hear how that was concluded? Great! Hey check out the next chapter.

Paul and Peter on Spiritual DNA
Chapter 2

Do you know why many of Paul's writings were in Greek? It was due to Hellenization. Hellenization (or Hellenisation) is a historical term widely used to describe the cultural influence on civilizations that

 became Hellenized. It was most prominently achieved under Alexander III of Macedon who spread Greek culture, language and religion throughout the lands he conquered. The results were devastating to the lands and providences he conquered, leaving

elements of Greek origin and influence merging in varying degrees with elements from the vanquished civilizations, with the dominant influence lying in the hands of the Greek victors; ultimately sublimating and consuming the captive, vanquished and vanishing culture. This is known as Hellenism.

Once the land was conquered and controlled the Greek Diaspora would follow with many Greeks migrating to these lands and occupying its territory by the masses. Now what made Hellenism unique was that the occupants did not change the name of the territory they conquered. They would simply adopt the name and citizenry of such providence.

In the Hellenistic times, the Macedonians, following the death of Alexander, Hellenized the Syrians, Jews, Egyptians, Persians, Armenians and a number of other smaller ethnic groups along the Middle East and Central Asia.

The Grecian Jews (or should I say the Hellenistic Greeks) conquered the Jewish community and through combining their culture and religion created a new culture along with the local Hebraic Jews who remained. The Hebraic Jews or should I say the Hebrews (who had been released from Egypt's grasp), had colonized that territory earlier in history by conquering the Canaanites. But pay close attention to the personalities of the Hellenistic Grecians and the attributes of the rulers of the Jewish people in Jerusalem.

The spirit of such an action leaves one to inquire why people continue to treat the ruling powers of Jerusalem as if they were the chosen people of the past when the prominent occupants were and still to this day are of Greek origin.

Here let me bring it closer to home for you. Similar to the European colonization of the Americas, the land was widely populated by people we know as the American Indians. Now unlike the descendants of Alexander the Greats' Hellenization of the Jews in Israel, the European conquest of the Americas had more of a Roman Empire flare. The Europeans conquered the Native American Indians and did not adopt their Indian tribal names nor did they rule from within. Now if you were to ask a descendant of European colonists whether he felt that he was less of an American than the Native American Indian, he would look at you like you were crazy. In fact there is a high probability that he would feel far more American than any of the Native Indians because of the evolving culture of America as we know it today.

Are you making a connection yet? So when we look at the Jewish people of yesterday, philosophizing and discussing scriptures in the synagogue similar to the Greek philosophers back in Athens, we can understand from their Hellenistic ancestry what these quasi rulers, the Pharisees and Sadducees were like. So, back in the days of the

31

Messiah and later in Paul's days their synagogues were full of Greeks and Hebrews, or Grecian Jews and Hebraic Jews (the Hebraic Jews being under the covenant of Abraham), which is touched on in Acts 6:

> And in those days, when the number of the disciples was multiplied, there arose a murmuring of the Grecians against the Hebrews, because their widows were neglected in the daily ministration. (Acts 6:1)

The Grecians were disgruntled? Well of course! They were looking for the same treatment for their widows as that being received by the Hebrew widows. They had adopted the faith and wanted their portions.

In Revelation the Messiah states:

> **I know thy works, and tribulation, and poverty, (but thou art rich) and [I know] the blasphemy of them which say they are Jews, and are not, but [are] the synagogue of Satan.**
> (Revelation 2:9)

We have some Ministers today misquoting scriptures, pledging allegiance to Israel and coercing their congregations to revere the Jews in power over them today, while the congregations believe that they are revering the Hebrew nation to which the covenant was given.

I have not come for you, but for the lost sheep of Israel. Remember that statement?

How many times have I heard from Christians that they could not understand how the Jews could not see or understand that Jesus was the Messiah? How a nation of people that came out of worshiping pagan gods, Hellenic polytheism (meaning many gods such as in Greek Mythology, which is mostly practiced among the Wiccan religion better know as witch craft to this very day)--how could these Pharisees not accept what the Messiah was saying?

 If being one of the chosen ones is of a physical nature versus a spiritual nature, then why is it that the proclaimed chosen Jews refuse to believe that the Messiah has come? In 1991, why did the Israeli government spend their resources and fly down to Ethiopia to gather Ethiopian Jews (Hebrews) in a covert operation known by the name of **Operation Solomon,** a 36 hour non-stop mass exodus of the Ethiopian Jews to Israel? Over 14,000 flown in on a convoy of IAF C130's planes landing back and forth and even stuffing a 747 (shown here) to the extent of 1,122 passengers? These covert missions were executed by the government of Israel beginning with Operation Moses, and Operation Joshua.

First, Operation Moses took place in 1984 with over 8,000 Ethiopian Jews coming from Sudan. Listen to who assisted Israel via these covert missions. I'm sorry, did I say covert? The entire operation was a cooperative effort between the Israeli Defense Forces, the Central Intelligence Agency, the United States Embassy in Khartoum, mercenaries and Sudanese State Security Forces.

Second, in 1985 was a follow-up operation, Operation Joshua. Who do you think was involved? George H. W. Bush, the Vice-President of the United States at the time, arranged a CIA-sponsored follow-up mission to Operation Moses. Under Operation Joshua, an additional 800 were flown out of Sudan to Israel. But in the following five years, all efforts on behalf of the Beta Israel fell on the closed ears of Mengistu Haile Mariam's dictatorship. As soon as the dictator loss power in 1991 Operation Solomon engaged and the 14,000 plus Ethiopians previously mentioned were transported.

George H. Bush helped Israel secure these Jews and bring them to Israel. George Bush's son became President of the United States at a later date. Well he really didn't win the election, but he became President never the less and when prompted about helping suffering African nations, George W. Bush, Jr. stated, "We are not a nation of nation builders. We cannot help everyone or interfere with everything." So that means no help for Darfur, Sudan, Rwanda, and the list continues. But what a concerted effort by the United State and Israel! I have not seen the Israeli government go into any other

33

country with such aggression and ship over people who called themselves Jews. But these people were special; they worshiped God in the original manner dating back to King Solomon and beyond. Did I tell you that this was a covert mission? I wonder what they wanted them for; probably to tie up some loose ends.

Are you getting the picture yet? You see, I need to give you a background of the mindset of these people that the Messiah was in continual confrontation with. It's important to separate the humbleness of the Hebrews and the aggression of the Hellenistic Grecian Jews. When you hear the words "Crucify him!" you can kind of put it in better perspective now. In Acts chapter 13 Paul was beginning his ministry and found himself bumping up against the same wall of aggression as the Messiah:

> And when the Jews were gone out of the synagogue, the Gentiles besought that these words might be preached to them the next sabbath.
>
> Now when the congregation was broken up, many of the Jews and religious proselytes followed Paul and Barnabas: who, speaking to them, persuaded them to continue in the grace of God.
> (Acts 13:42-43)

Notice how the Grecian Jews and Hebrew Jews were both in the synagogue while Paul and Barnabas were speaking, but the Gentiles were lured and moved by Paul's sayings. **(Now pay close attention; this was an important passage)** With the efforts of Paul and Barnabas to spread the gospel, some of the crowd did not accept it and others did. Mind you, we are dealing with the assortment of Jews. The Diaspora had occurred over a century before the birth of The Messiah, not to mention Paul's journeys, so we are dealing with generations of crossbreeds, Spiritual DNA, not physical, but similar to what Jesus stated in the gospel of John 8:43 **Why do ye not understand my speech? [even] because ye cannot hear my word.** Even among the Jews, there are many who receive the gospel because of their Spiritual DNA. It continues:

34

> *And the next sabbath day came almost*
> *the whole city together to hear the word*
> *of God.*
>
> *But when the Jews saw the multitudes,*
> *they were filled with envy, and spake*
> *against those things which were spoken*
> *by Paul, contradicting and blaspheming.*
>
> *Then Paul and Barnabas waxed bold,*
> *and said, It was necessary that the word*
> *of God should first have been spoken to*
> *you: but seeing ye put it from you, and*
> *judge yourselves unworthy of everlasting*
> *life, lo, we turn to the Gentiles. (Acts 13:44-*
> *46)*

Here Paul and Barnabas identified their mission to the isles of the Gentiles--to speak the gospel and see who the gospel would resonate with. Paul found himself caught between more than one world, but passion still flowed from him whether he was ministering to the Jewish community or to the Europeans (Gentiles).

Paul wrote many letters; some were sent through Timothy and others directly to the communities of the cities where they dwelled. In his letters to the believers in Corinth, Paul addresses the relationship between husband and wife as it relates to one of the spouses being a non-believer and what their fate would be. Now mind you, Paul continued to be questioned about many things that were not touched on in the scriptures or the writings of the gospels.

> *But to the rest speak I, not the Lord: If any*
> *brother hath a wife that believeth not,*
> *and she be pleased to dwell with him, let*
> *him not put her away.*

> And the woman which hath an husband
> that believeth not, and if he be pleased
> to dwell with her, let her not leave him.
>
> For the unbelieving husband is sanctified
> by the wife, and the unbelieving wife is
> sanctified by the husband: else were your
> children unclean; but now are they holy.
> (1 Corinthians 7:12-14)

Now when Paul writes a letter to Timothy, he states that the woman who was deceived by Satan from the beginning is not able to be saved unless she be saved in childbearing, if her children...:

> And Adam was not deceived, but the
> woman being deceived was in the
> transgression.
>
> Notwithstanding she shall be saved in
> childbearing, if they continue in faith and
> charity and holiness with sobriety. (1
> Timothy 2:14-15)

Was this a contradiction? Read it for yourself. Women are saved through childbearing only if the child does such and such? What if this was **just a letter to Timothy**. Can you say, "Letter to Timothy"? Was Paul chauvinistic? Many scholars think so. Could chauvinism show up in the Bible and not be inspired by God? Just an opinion, but, of course Paul and Timothy have had many conversations about such accounts, so Paul wrote a letter, his opinion, to Timothy. So you have possible contradictions, opinions, inspired statements from God and so on. If you want to control the masses you will state "Hey it's all inspired from God". Case closed. Don't question it. In Second Peter 1:20-21 Peter states:

> Knowing this first, that no prophecy of the
> scripture is of any private interpretation.
>
> For the prophecy came not in old time by
> the will of man: but holy men of God
> spake [as they were] moved by the Holy
> Ghost. (2 Peter 1:20-21)

Paul and Peter did not refer to their own letters as "scriptures". Hey, what are the scriptures? Name the books that comprised the scriptures...if you were back in Paul's day, that is. Name the books that comprised the scriptures and remember the New Testament was not a part of the scriptures yet, which is why it's called the New Testament. You must ask who, what, when, where and why.

This brings us to something very important: Who decided what books would go into the compilation of the 66 books of the Bible in the first place, deeming **all** of them to be called "scripture"? Examining this before going any further may prove to be very valuable before we go on parroting what we have been told. Let's find out what is and isn't true by further examination:

You have 46 books in the Old Testament, which, according to Hebrew Bible, consist of three sections: the Torah, Nevi'im and Ketuvim.

Tanakh (Hebrew: ד״נת) is an acronym that identifies the Hebrew Bible. The acronym is formed from the initial Hebrew letters of the Tanakh's three traditional subdivisions:

Torah (הרות), meaning "teaching" or "law," includes the Five Books of Moses. The printed form of the Torah is called "the Chumash" (שמוח), meaning "five-part." The Torah is also known by its Greek name, "the Pentateuch," which similarly means "five scrolls."

Nevi'im (םיאיבנ), meaning "Prophets." This division includes the books which, as a whole, cover the chronological era from the entrance of the Israelites into the Land until the Babylonian captivity of Judah (the "period of prophecy"). However, they exclude Chronicles, which covers the same period. The Nevi'im are often divided into the Earlier Prophets, which are generally historical, and the Later Prophets, which contain more exhorted, cautionary prophecies and admonishments.

Ketuvim (םיבותכ), meaning "Writings," are sometimes also known by the Greek title "Hagiographa." These encompass all the remaining books, and include the Five Scrolls. They are sometimes also divided into such categories as the "wisdom books" of Job, Ecclesiastes, and Proverbs, the "poetry books" of Psalms, Lamentations and Song of Solomon, and the "historical books" of Ezra, Nehemiah and Chronicles.

The term "Old Testament" was never intended to be considered a pejorative term. It was viewed as an aggregate, not to be replaced by the New Testament. It came from the Christian theologian Tertullian who used the Latin word, testamentum. This was a Latin translation of the Greek word diatheke (covenant). In the LXX, diatheke is the word used in Jeremiah 31:33-34 to refer to YHWH's Covenant.

Quintus Septimius Florens Tertullianus, anglicized as Tertullian(ca. 155–230), was a church leader and prolific author of Early Christianity. He also was a notable early Christian apologist. Tertullian, a Romanized African, was born, lived and died in Carthage, in what is today Tunisia. Tertullian denounced Christian doctrines as he considered them heretical, but later in life adopted views that themselves came to be regarded as heretical. Imagine that. He was the first great writer of Latin Christianity, thus sometimes known as the "Father of the Latin Church". He introduced the term Trinity (Theophilius to Autolycus {ca.115-181},introduced the word Trinity in his Book 2, Chapter 15 on the creation of the 4th day) as the Latin trinitas, to the Christian vocabulary and also probably the formula "three Persons, one Substance" as the Latin "tres Personae, una Substantia". Are you able to see the difference between what is inspired and what is interpreted in this example?

The Torah ("Teaching") [also known as the Pentateuch/Humash] consists of:
1. Genesis [בראשית / B'reshit]
2. Exodus [תומש / Sh'mot]
3. Leviticus [ויקרא / Vayiqra]
4. Numbers [במדבר / B'midbar]
5. Deuteronomy [דברים / D'varim]

The books of Nevi'im ("Prophets") are:
6. Joshua [יהושע / Y'hoshua]
7. Judges [שופטים / Shophtim]
8. Samuel (I & II) [שמואל / Sh'muel]

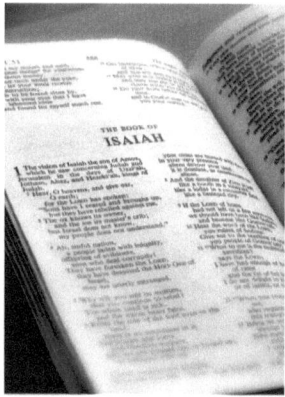

9. Kings (I & II) [מלכים / M'lakhim]
10. Isaiah [ישעי / Y'shayahu]
11. Jeremiah [ירמיה / Yir'mi'yahu]
12. Ezekiel [יחזקאל / Y'khezqel]
13. The Twelve Minor Prophets [תרי עשר]
    I. Hosea [הושע / Hoshea]
    II. Joel [יואל / Yo'el]
    III. Amos [עמוס / Amos]
    IV. Obadiah [עובדיה / Ovadyah]
    V. Jonah [יונה / Yonah]
    VI. Micah [מיכה / Mikhah]
    VII. Nahum [נחום / Nakhum]
    VIII. Habakkuk [חבקוק /Khavaquq]
    IX. Zephaniah [צפניה / Ts'phanyah]
    X. Haggai [יגח / Khagai]
    XI. Zechariah [זכריה / Z'kharyah]
    XII. Malachi [מלאכי / Mal'akhi]

The <u>Ketuvim</u> ("Writings") are:
14. Psalms [תהלים / T'hilim]
15. Proverbs [משלי / Mishlei]
16. Job [איוב / Iyov]
17. Song of Songs [שיר השירים / Shir Hashirim]
18. Ruth [רות / Rut]
19. Lamentations [איכה / Eikhah]
20. Ecclesiastes [קהלת / Qohelet]
21. Esther [אסתר / Est(h)er]
22. Daniel [דניאל / Dani'el]
23. Ezra-Nehemiah [עזרא ונחמיה / Ezra wuNekhem'ya]
24. Chronicles (I & II) [דברי הימים / Divrey Hayamim]

The Authorized King James Version is an English translation of the Christian Bible by the Church of England. Its work began in 1604 and was first published in 1611. It was common for it to take so long, as was the case with most other translations of the period. The New Testament was translated from the Textus Receptus (Received Text) series of the Greek texts.

Now that's disturbing. How do you go from the Messiah who spoke mostly Aramaic to his surroundings **(note: We all know the Messiah could speak what ever language he wanted)**, to texts and books that were written in Greek and authors unknown but assumed to be ....

The Old Testament was translated from the Masoretic Hebrew text, while the Apocrypha was translated from the Greek Septuagint (LXX).

The 1611 Bible is known as the King James Version in the United States. In the United Kingdom, it is commonly known as the Authorized Version. Neither name is superior. King James did not literally translate the Bible, but it was his advanced authorization that was legally necessary for the Church of England to translate, publish and distribute the Bible in England.

Most Christians (Protestant, Baptist, and so on) if questioned, will tell you that they do not subscribe to Catholicism. But these same people read from a Bible assembled by Catholics, authorized by the King. Here, let me give you more information on it--let's go back a bit. In May 1601, King James VI of Scotland attended the General Assembly of the Church of Scotland at St. Columbus's Church in Burntisland, Fife, and proposals were put forward for a new translation of the Bible into English. There was a lot of finger pointing and accusation going on, accusing the Church of reinterpreting the Bible to suit the needs of the Church and not translate the gospels as they were intended to be written. So King James proposed a new translation be commissioned to settle the controversies in hopes that a new translation would replace the **Geneva Bible** and its offensive notes, which were in the popular esteem. (The Geneva Bible had many inserts and suggestions of conduct, similar to Paul's writings. Neither were regarded as Holy Scripture, but as interpretations of what certain gospels and writings meant.)

King James gave the translators instructions that were designed to discourage polemical notes, to eliminate controversy and to guarantee that the new version would conform to the ecclesiology of the Church of England.

King James' actual instructions included the following requirements:

> The ordinary Bible, read in the church, commonly called the **Bishops' Bible**, was to be followed and as minimally altered as the original will permit....

> The old ecclesiastical words were to be kept; as in the word "church", not to be translated to "congregation". When any word hath diverse   significations, that which was to be kept would be that which has been most commonly used by the most eminent fathers, being agreeable to the propriety of the place, and the analogy of the faith....

> No marginal notes at all to be affixed, with the exception of the explanations of the Hebrew or Greek words, which cannot, without some circumlocution, so briefly and fitly be expressed in the text.

> Such quotations of places to be marginally set down, shall serve for the fit references of one scripture to another.

> These translations to be used when they agree better with the text than the **Bishops' Bible**, viz. **Tyndale Bible, Coverdale Bible, Matthew's Bible, Great Bible, Geneva Bible**. (Influence from **Taverner's Bible** and the New Testament of the **Douai-Rheims Bible** can also be detected, but the **Douai Old Testament** was published too late to have any effect.)

King James' instructions made it clear that he wanted the resulting translation to contain a **minimum of**

controversial notes and apparatus, and that he wanted the **episcopal structure of the Established Church**, and **traditional beliefs about an ordained clergy to be reflected** in the new translation.

Now do you see why it's called the King James Version? Obviously, the King had to step up to stop the continued Hellenization of the Bible. You thought Hellenization stopped back in the day, way back in history. Not! It continues even unto this day.

His order directed the translators to revise the **Bishop's Bible**, comparing other named English versions. It is for this reason that the flyleaves of most printings of the King James Bible observe that the text had been "translated out of the original tongues and with the former translations diligently compared and revised (by His Majesty's special command.)"

The Authorized Version was translated by 47 scholars (although 54 were originally contracted) working in six committees, based two each in the universities of Oxford, Cambridge and Westminster.
These Universities bear the exact names of the gentlemen who translated the Bible with their efforts to end the controversy between such different translations.

Controversy surrounded the canons, or should I say the list of books to be included (and their translations), and was appropriately fueled by the same methods used to control the masses by using individuals who were strongly against the Church and State's present efforts to continue such practices.

For example, in 1535 Myles Coverdale (shown above) published the first complete English Bible in print, the so-called **Coverdale Bible**. As *Coverdale was not proficient in Hebrew or Greek*, he used 'five sundry interpreters' in Latin, English and 'Deutsch' (German) as source text. He made use of Tyndale's translation of the New Testament (following Tyndale's November 1534 Antwerp edition) and of those books which were translated by Tyndale: the Pentateuch, and the book of Jonah.

John Wycliffe (pictured here) felt that all Christians should have access to the Bible in the vernacular (tongue of the Land). He is credited with being the first to give a complete translation of the Bible into English (called Wycliffe's Bible), in 1382. He was one of the first individuals to speak out against the Church amassing such phenomenal wealth. He was very outspoken about the Church treating the word of God as the early apostles did. He felt uncomfortable about the way Church and State merged in efforts to control the masses. He was probably considered (by the church) to be radical and heretical. It's important to recognize the origin of such authorities.

Before we go spouting "the whole 66 books are the scriptures", we might want to continue this historical detour before commenting further on the writings of Paul and Peter.

The New Testament (Greek: Καινὴ Διαθήκη, Kainē Diathēkē) is the name given to the final portion of the Christian Bible, written after the Old Testament. It is sometimes called the Greek Testament or Greek Scriptures, or the New Covenant – which is the literal translation of the original Greek. The original texts were written in Koine Greek by various unknown authors after c. AD 45 and before c. AD 140. Its 27 books were gradually collected into a single volume over a period of several centuries. The New Testament is a central element of Christianity, and has played a major role in shaping modern Western culture.

In ancient times there were dozens of Christian writings claiming apostolic authorship, or for some other reason considered to have authority by some ancient churches, but they were ultimately excluded from the 27-book New Testament canon {list}.

Each of the gospels narrates the ministry of Jesus of Nazareth. The traditional author is listed after each entry. Modern scholars differ on precisely by whom, when, or in what original form the various gospels were written. You know for something to be held in such esteem, there are just too many ghost writers. Something is not right about that. Unfortunately, even the gospels have challenges in authorship, but they are the closest thing to the true ministry of the Messiah than anything else in the 66 books called the Bible.

The Gospel of Matthew is traditionally ascribed to the Apostle Matthew, son of Alphaeus.
The Gospel of Mark is traditionally ascribed to Mark the Evangelist, who wrote down the recollections of the Apostle Simon Peter.
The Gospel of Luke is traditionally ascribed to Luke, a physician and companion of Saul of Tarsus (Paul).
The Gospel of John is traditionally ascribed to the Apostle John, son of Zebedee.

The first three are commonly classified as the Synoptic Gospels. They contain very similar accounts of events in the Messiah's life. The Gospel of John stands apart for its unique records of several miracles and sayings of the Messiah, not found elsewhere.

The Pauline epistles typically refer to the thirteen New Testament books which have been traditionally ascribed to the Apostle Paul. Among them are some of the earliest extant Christian documents. They provide an insight into the beliefs and controversies of formative Christianity and as part of the canon of the New Testament, they have also been (and continue to be) huge influence in Christian theology and ethics. Some of them are probably the earliest New Testament documents, with the exception of those in which the

Hebrews have presented Paul as the author. The epistle to the Hebrews is something of a special case, being anonymous. Authorship of Hebrews has been disputed from its beginning and few modern scholars would attribute it to Paul. Thus some classifications do not include Hebrews as a Pauline epistle, listing it instead with the general epistles.

Hey, how are you holding up? Good I suspect. If you got this far you have proven yourself to be one who is genuinely interested in finding out what the Messiah meant by "He that has an ear, let him hear." With only a small background on the origin of the construction of the Bible (and believe me it was a small synopsis), a whole lot more is to be gained, and since we can establish such, well let's continue.

What kept resurfacing was the dispute and controversy of the authorship and authentication of scriptures. Hey, the Messiah knows best. That is the one thing we know for a fact. Or do we? All of the additional supporting dialogue, well, it's good for reproof and a measuring stick for conduct. As I told you earlier and I'll tell you again, "Red letter trumps all". So when you have the writers expounding on issues that seem chauvinistic, or that you should martyr your flesh, just keep it in its proper context, ok?

You see, the word "epistle" is from the Greek word epistolos which means a written "letter" addressed to a recipient or recipients, perhaps part of exchanged correspondence. Today in common usage this somewhat elevated term usually connotes a specific group of books in the New Testament that were either letters or were written in that literary format, although "epistle" can refer to other written missives as well, such as a bishop's open letter to the congregants of his churches. Calling a letter an "epistle" does not in and of itself imply that the letter is part of the New Testament, inspired, or even that it is necessarily religious in nature. For instance, an epistolary novel is told in the form of a series of letters.

In c. 380 AD, after many attempts to perfect what would be heard and the anticipated effect subsequent teachings would have on the masses, a redactor of the Apostolic Constitutions was issued by the current Pope of the time (Clement), including a canon which would be attributed directly to the Twelve Apostles as the **85th** of his **list** of such apostolic decrees: **Canon 85**, which would be the method used for determining what would be taught and entered into the church liturgy. Canon 85 read; "Let the following books be esteemed venerable and holy by all of you, both clergy and laity." He was referring to the list of books of the Old Testament--our **sacred books;** the New Testament: the four gospels of **Matthew**, **Mark**, **Luke**, **John**, the fourteen Epistles of Paul (which included Hebrews), two epistles from Peter, three from John, one from James, one from Jude and two epistles from Clement; the Constitutions dedicated to the bishops by the Pope: eight books, which are **not appropriate** to make public before all, because of the mysteries contained in them; and the **Acts of us**, the **Apostles**.

The Pope of the Catholic Church waved his magic wand and proclaimed the letters or epistles of Paul and Peter and John to be considered as the Holy Scriptures. A man did this, not God. A man with the influence of the growing theocracy converted letters into scriptures giving the world "Pauline Christianity". A mere man who many people of today call a man with the same title of Pope, "Holy Father" or "Your Holiness". Stop it people. He is a man who is not the Messiah, not God, not the Creator, not omnipresent and not omnipotent enough to be revered as Holy Father. Remember in the first letter from Peter that Peter himself referred to previous writings as scripture and now a man claiming to be God has taken this letter from Peter and deemed it a "holy scripture".

The term Pauline Christianity refers to a branch of Early Christianity associated with the beliefs and doctrines espoused by Paul the Apostle through his writings. Most of mainstream Christianity relies heavily on these suggestions by Paul, refer to them as teachings, and consider them to be amplifications and explanations of the teachings of the Messiah. Others perceive in Paul's writings teachings that are radically different from the original teachings of the Messiah, which are documented in the canonical gospels, early Acts and the rest of the New Testament, such as the Epistle of James.

Proponents of the perceived Pauline distinctive include Marcion of Sinope, the 2nd century theologian who asserted that Paul was the only apostle who had rightly understood the new message of salvation as delivered by the Messiah. Opponents of the same era include the Ebonite's and Nazarenes, who rejected Paul for straying from "normative" Judaism. Now in the Messiah's own words, according to Matthew 15:24:

> *I am not sent but unto the lost sheep of the house of Israel.*

So you have the Ebionites, the Nazarenes, and many of the early Christians who worked to spread the words of the gospel to the masses left feeling totally disconnected from Pauline Christianity.

Pauline Christianity as an expression first came into use in the twentieth century amongst those scholars who proposed different strands of thought within Early Christianity, where Paul was a powerful influence. It has since come into widespread use amongst non-Christian scholars and depends on the claim advanced in different ages, that not only is the form of the faith found in the writings of Paul radically different from that found elsewhere in the New Testament, but also that his influence came to predominate. Reference is also made to the large number of non-canonical texts, some of which

46

have been discovered during the last hundred years and show the many movements and strands of thought emanating from the Messiah's life and teachings or even possibly contemporary to them--some of which can be contrasted with Paul's thought. Ebionism and Gnosticism are two of the more significant, however there is no universal agreement as to Gnosticism's relationship to either Christianity in general or the writings of Paul in particular.

Now that you have a more expanded view of the letters of Paul and Peter, and you know the motivation for choosing which books will be taught and you know who structured the list of books in Canon #85, we need to look at one more important fact about the canonized King James versus of the Bible. Are there more books that aren't included in Canon #85? Of course there are! So when you hear someone tell you, "The Bible is all you need," they are not telling you the truth.

You see, other Christians have been polarized by the propaganda of promoting the infallible word. Let's take a closer look at what man calls the word of God and what God calls the word of God. Crystalline truth goes beyond a Pope canonizing or a King authorizing what is "holy". It is "truth", untainted by man's hands or deceit. Let's look at things that supersede man's interpretation. There are laws, powers and principalities that exist. Every law may not be documented within the 66 books of Canon #85. Every book that is holy is definitely not in the 66 books listed in the King James Bible. For example: The Book of Life. Now the Book of Life is referenced in Canon #85 but the Book of Life is not included within the 66 books and to our knowledge this book is not located anywhere on this earth.

Could there be other books documenting laws, powers and restrictions that may not be contained within the 66 books in addition to the Book of Life, that are not on this earth? After all, God is so broad in scope that he did make heavens and the earth. So why not then? Why can't there be other books? It seems plausible. There are things about heavenly places that we just don't know. But we do get clues, hints, and sneak previews.

Given that foundation, I'll pose a question. In Matthew 4:1-11 the Messiah and the devil were conversing back and forth like two attorneys. The Messiah commented back and forth with references to what was written and Satan countered with responses that that also referenced what was written. Both reached for legal endorsement of their view point by stating, "It is written". Now to what writings are they referring? Are they referencing writings from the 66 books of Canon #85? Is Satan bound by the inspired writing of man such as the Old Testament? Or is Satan bound by laws, powers and restrictions which precede and pre-date these writings? When they shouted back and forth, "It is written," were they referring to writings not from this world? If so, the "it is written" could be referencing that which supersedes the inspired writings of man that later became known as "the scriptures".

There are so many documents that exist on earth and beyond that are not included among the **received texts** of the **Catholic church**: the book of Maccabees, the book of Enoch, the book of the Watchers and hey, if you want to throw letters into the mix then check out what the epistles of Clement, Polycarp, Barnabas, etc. are about. Go right ahead!

Some scholars would share that the Messiah and Satan were referring to Deuteronomy, or some other book written by Moses. If Satan were bound by the writings of man, then all we would need to do is write a book were he loses immediately and stop worrying about him. Bind Satan up immediately in these **new** scriptures, have the Pope canonize **this** book and save a lot of people from Satan's wrath and the world will be at peace. But, we can't do that can we, because man's writing of such things doesn't bind Satan that easily, does it?

In the book of Acts a person thought they could bind a demon and cast it out by merely saying "in the name of Jesus..." The man approached this situation in the same manner that some scholars would have--by referencing scriptures inaccurately to justify an origin. Check out what happened in a similar situation:

> *Then certain of the vagabond Jews,*
> *exorcists, took upon them to call over*
> *them which had evil spirits the name of*
> *the Lord Jesus, saying, We adjure you by*
> *Jesus whom Paul preacheth.*
>
> *And there were seven sons of [one]*
> *Sceva, a Jew, [and] chief of the priests,*
> *which did so.*

*And the evil spirit answered and said,
Jesus I know, and Paul I know; but who
are ye?*

*And the man in whom the evil spirit was
leaped on them, and overcame them,
and prevailed against them, so that they
fled out of that house naked and
wounded.*

*And this was known to all the Jews and
Greeks also dwelling at Ephesus; and fear
fell on them all, and the name of the Lord
Jesus was magnified.*

*And many that believed came, and
confessed, and shewed their deeds.*

*Many of them also which used curious
arts brought their books together, and
burned them before all [men]: and they
counted the price of them, and found [it]
fifty thousand [pieces] of silver. (Acts
19:13-19)*

As you may know by now, this is not a Christian inspirational. I'm not
sharing with you, my assistant, misleading words of inspiration, but I
will work hard to reveal the truth to you. Let the truth inspire you. We
are not alone. There has been an ongoing feast of lies and
misdirection perpetrated by ministers and church leaders. Although
many of them have been unintentional, there are also many in the
pulpit who mean well, but are not qualified by the spirit to lead or
teach.

If churches continue to propagate the recruitment of individuals who
are not the lost sheep, you will continue to have wolves in sheep's
clothing misleading the masses. When you look at the letters Paul
wrote to the different churches, he attempted, to the best of his
ability, to describe Spiritual DNA. He felt the duality of his existence,
just like many of you, but in Paul's case he wrote of crucifying the
flesh. Although he saw the flesh as the alter ego, flesh is not bad.
Back in Genesis when God made everything, among the things

included when he "saw that it was good", was man. I have not found any writing where the Messiah said anything bad about flesh. Your flesh won't stand trial. Your human soul will. Your flesh is just a biological machine that assists you in experiencing this flux world. You don't have to martyr your flesh or work in disharmony with yourself like a madman arguing with yourself in private. Again, nowhere in the writings did the Messiah say the flesh is bad or martyr it. Writings that do state such are all within the letters of Paul or Peter. Remember that what the Messiah said is more important. Many individuals search for Christian inspirational books to endorse their views and already preconceived notions of whom and what they are in the Messiah. I'm not here to pat you on the back. The best way I can show love to my fellow believers is to tell the truth.

The Christian view of Jesus carries more weight than organized religion often presents. The arguments, the back and forth referencing, the "who reflects his teachings most accurately?" to what should be studied by the laity are concepts that all stem from the original Hebrew theocratic belief in a Kingdom of God with spiritual beings in human bodies having a human experience.

You have overwhelming and irrefutable evidence in the information that has been shared with you. The New Testament became the Holy Scriptures because a Catholic Pope waved a wand and pronounced them Holy in canon #85. You see, there is an overwhelming amount of evidence of the stolen legacy of the Hebrews through the Hellenization process brought by the Greeks. There have been covert operations executed in the name of... sanctioned by... Why do you think that most of the New Testament was interpreted from the Greek and not Hebrew? Why do most Israelites send their children to school to learn to read Hebrew? Why? Because it's Hebrew they claim as their native tongue. You have letters from Paul (of whom I am a big fan), but come on, put them in their proper prospective: they were letters, he was giving advice. Many people have written letters or epistles that were not canonized because their letters did not serve the church in promoting the submission of the believer to the church. Forget submitting to God! According to the church, "submit to the church or die," which is something we will be covering next along with more information on the evil ones while going to the heart of Spiritual DNA. Why did the Messiah continue to say **"He that has an ear, let him hear"**?

The Kingdom vs. The Church
Chapter 3

And saying, The time is fulfilled, and the kingdom of God is at hand: repent ye, and believe the gospel. (Mark 1:15)

Again, the kingdom of heaven is like unto a net, that was cast into the sea, and gathered of every kind:

Which, when it was full, they drew to shore, and sat down, and gathered the good into vessels, but cast the bad away.

So shall it be at the end of the world: the angels shall come forth, and sever the wicked from among the just,

And shall cast them into the furnace of fire: there shall be wailing and gnashing of teeth. (Matthew 13:47-50)

Is there a difference between the Kingdom and the Church? Oh yeah. The **Kingdom of God** (<u>Greek</u>: - *Basileia tou Theou,*) is a foundational concept in Christianity, as it is the central theme of Jesus the Christ's message in the Synoptic Gospels. The phrase occurs in the New Testament more than 100 times. According to the Messiah, the Kingdom of God is among the people. Is it "realized eschatology"? Some believe it's largely based on Luke 11:20, and Luke 17:21 claiming that "the kingdom of God has come to you" and "the kingdom of God is within you".

John Crossan, one of the co-founders of the Jesus Seminar, imagined Jesus as a somewhat cynical peasant who focused on the sapiential (offering wisdom) aspects of the "Kingdom" and not on any apocalyptic conceptions.

While others, Norman Perrin, Albert Schweitzer, Johannes Weiss, and Rudolf Bultmann argued that the Messiah's "Kingdom" was intended to be a wholly futuristic kingdom. These scholars looked to the apocalyptic traditions of various Jewish groups existing at the time of the Messiah. They approached the character of the Messiah from the viewpoint of a human and not that of a divine being. They looked at him as a preacher-turned-prophet who improperly predicted the end of the ages. From this perspective, the Messiah was an apocalyptic preacher who would bring about the end times and when he did not see the end of the cosmic order coming, he embraced death as a tool to provoke God into action.

It's interesting how some could take such a view. What man could provoke God into action? The Messiah? The same Messiah that stated to Satan, **Thou shall not tempt the Lord thy God?** But they believed he was a whining brat who improperly predicted the end of the ages and thus martyred himself to spite God and provoke God into action. Sounds kind of Hellenistic to me--more methods to distort the truth--but according to scholars…. Well the scholars…. This leads directly to why I have problems with leading authorities in the scriptures, or anyone who taught me or anyone else about reading "their" material, as if the road to GOD exclusively goes through "them". How about requesting that people read and research for themselves?

That's why I continue to encourage you, my assistant and readers, to read for yourselves. Don't take anyone's word for anything.

The Kingdom of God is what the Messiah says it is and is sometimes even reiterated by other authors, such as Paul, Polycarp, and others. Sometimes is the key word like in the scripture above. Matthew 13:47-50 states that the Kingdom consists of everything: good and bad individuals. But it is regulated by the decisions of God and, according to the scripture; there is an appointed time for the separation of the Lost Sheep and the evil ones.

Again, the word "Kingdom" is a translation of the Greek word "basileia", which in turn is a translation of the words "malkuth" (Hebrew) and "malkutha" (Aramaic). The words in Hebrew and Aramaic do not define kingdom by territory, but by dominion. Some say that reading any translation of Canon #85 is okay. Not so. The difference between an Empire (basileia) and Dominance (malkutha) is huge.

According to the writings the Messiah said of the Kingdom of God that one cannot say, "Look here it is!" or "There it is!" (Luke 17:21). According to C.H. Dodd, the common translation of "malkuth" in Hebrew is with "basileia" in Greek and hence "Kingdom" in English is therefore problematic; a translation with "kingship," "kingly rule," "reign" or "sovereignty" would be preferable. From a purely etymological viewpoint, the word "basileia" is believed to have been derived from the Greek word for base or foundation. Some writers prefer this root definition because it eliminates the confusion with monarchy. Scholars during the current third quest for the historical Messiah have translated the phrase "Kingdom of God" as "God's imperial rule", or sometimes "God's domain", to better grasp its sense in today's language.

The premise of a Kingdom is integral to both Jewish and Christian Scriptures. The Hebrew Bible (synonymous with the Protestant Old Testament) contains a set of laws, known as The Law, which governed the nation of Israel as a Theocracy. Prophecies throughout the Old Testament refer to this Kingdom as esoteric in nature, or spiritual, later revealed to be fulfilled through King David's lineage.

So when we say Kingdom we mean dominance. In stating so, let's deal with the nature of the Kingdom or what is considered to be the true essence of the Kingdom. You have individuals who are alive and individuals who are dead. Very simple, don't you think?

Now life means everlasting, and death means separation. Your life is your spirit. It just so happens that your spirit is in your body--well, at least for right now. Your spirit will live forever, but whether or not you will be counted among the living spirits or the dead spirits is the question. Both life and death fall under the dominion of the

Kingdom. Most scholars and ministers would teach that the Kingdom only possesses the living. But remember, Kingdom means dominance, or King Dominance, and God has dominance over the living and the dead as demonstrated in the verses below:

> **And I say unto you, That many shall come from the east and west, and shall sit down with Abraham, and Isaac, and Jacob, in the kingdom of heaven.**
>
> **But the children of the kingdom shall be cast out into outer darkness: there shall be weeping and gnashing of teeth.**
> *(Matthew 8:11-12)*
>
> **And fear not them which kill the body, but are not able to kill the soul: but rather fear him which is able to destroy both soul and body in hell.** *(Matthew 10:28)*

The children of the Kingdom shall be cast out into outer darkness? Why would the children of the Kingdom be cast out into outer darkness? Well, because the dominance or dominion of the King rules over the just and the unjust. The saved are the living spirits, the evil ones are the dead spirits and both are part of the Kingdom.

While Satan's kingdom is not in sovereignty, it is connected, but within the confines of God's Kingdom. If Satan's kingdom was separate and sovereign, it would not have to answer to God for anything. God would not have any governance; no power to overthrow; no authority to cast out; no means to tell any demon what to do. Can the French government tell an American citizen what to do while that individual is in America? I DON'T THINK SO! But the Federal government can tell any state in the union what to do because those states are subjected to a higher authority--a higher dominance. So, is the kingdom of Satan subjected to a higher authority and part of the union? As demonstrated in Job 1:6 while the visiting royalty were at the throne of God giving accountability for each of their kingdoms, Satan's turn presented itself:

> *Now there was a day when the sons of God came to present themselves before*

> the LORD, and Satan came also among
> them.
>
> And the LORD said unto Satan, Whence
> comest thou? Then Satan answered the
> LORD, and said, From going to and fro in
> the earth, and from walking up and down
> in it. (Job 1:6-7)

In case that went over your head, in Job 2:6 Satan returns on another day; did I say another day? He and the other sons of God came to present their reports to a **higher dominance**.

> Again there was a day when the sons of
> God came to present themselves before
> the LORD, and Satan came also among
> them to present himself before the LORD.
>
> And the LORD said unto Satan, From
> whence comest thou? And Satan
> answered the LORD, and said, From going
> to and fro in the earth, and from walking
> up and down in it.
>
> And the LORD said unto Satan, Hast thou
> considered my servant Job, that [there is]
> none like him in the earth, a perfect and
> an upright man, one that feareth God,
> and escheweth evil? and still he holdeth
> fast his integrity, although thou movedst
> me against him, to destroy him without
> cause.
>
> And Satan answered the LORD, and said,
> Skin for skin, yea, all that a man hath will
> he give for his life.
>
> But put forth thine hand now, and touch
> his bone and his flesh, and he will curse
> thee to thy face.

*And the LORD said unto Satan, Behold, he
[is] in thine hand; but save his life.*

*So went Satan forth from the presence of
the LORD, and smote Job with sore boils
from the sole of his foot unto his crown.
(Job 2:1-6)*

So as you see, we are not just caught up in a war of good vs. evil. We are caught up in a very magical world that is full of twists and turns as we participate in aggression between powers and principalities.

Within the Kingdom structure you have Henotheistic governance or powers, municipalities and might's. You heard right: Henotheistic governance, but a monotheistic Godhead or to say it plainly, God. God's definition (G.O.D. **G**eometrically **O**mnipresent *in all* **D**imensions) gives **him** total governance over all and **he** has empowered deities and established hierarchy within **his** Kingdom.

*And Jesus came and spake unto them,
saying, **All power is given unto me in
heaven and in earth.** (Matthew 28:18)*

What does this hierarchy consist of? Angels, and then you have archangels; laws and rules governing physics, and then things that are metaphysical; Satan, who has great power and might; Michael and Gabriel, both having many powers and mights, and then there are so many other angels and deities.

They all have dominion over many different things, or for a better word, they have kingdoms within the Kingdom. Do you remember when the Pharisees were accusing the Messiah of having demons in him enabling him to perform miracles? Do you remember the Messiah's response?

*And Jesus knew their thoughts, and said
unto them, **Every kingdom divided
against itself is brought to desolation; and
every city or house divided against itself
shall not stand:***

And if Satan cast out Satan, he is divided against himself; how shall then his kingdom stand? *(Matthew 12:25-26)*

A kingdom divided? Hmmmm. In Revelation there is another account of such Henotheistic governance:

> *These shall make war with the Lamb, and the Lamb shall overcome them: for he is Lord of lords, and King of kings: and they that are with him [are] called, and chosen, and faithful. (Revelation 17:14)*

King of kings and Lord of lords: Hmmmmm. Remember King Dominance or shall I say that the Messiah's King Dominance is a higher dominance then that of Satan's kingdom, or of the archangel Michael's (and for all those he rules over and commands). All kingdoms are a subset of the big Kingdom which is the Kingdom of God. In the book of Daniel this was stated about the Kingdom:

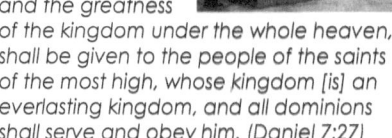

> *And the kingdom and dominion, and the greatness of the kingdom under the whole heaven, shall be given to the people of the saints of the most high, whose kingdom [is] an everlasting kingdom, and all dominions shall serve and obey him. (Daniel 7:27)*

Did you catch that: the saints of the most high; the highest ranking Kingdom; the Kingdom of Elohim? Once again, I will give you example after example because the obvious eludes many people and sometimes the many examples overshadow the repeated lies that have been perpetrated. In John 18 Pilate was inquiring about this Kingdom that the Jews had accused the Messiah of and he spoke again of coming for the Lost Sheep:

Jesus answered, **My kingdom is not of this world: if my kingdom were of this world, then would my servants fight, that I should not be delivered to the Jews: but now is my kingdom not from hence.**

Pilate therefore said unto him, Art thou a king then? Jesus answered, **Thou sayest that I am a king. To this end was I born, and for this cause came I into the world, that I should bear witness unto the truth. Every one that is of the truth heareth my voice.**

Pilate saith unto him, what is truth? And when he had said this, he went out again unto the Jews, and saith unto them, I find in him no fault [at all]. (John 18:36-37)

Everyone that is of the truth heareth my voice. Hmmmmm, can you say Lost Sheep? **I came to this world to bear witness unto the truth.** What could the Messiah possibly be sharing with the world that the world did not already know about his coming? Now here is wisdom for the "believer". If you ask many Christians today what the truth is, 95% will immediately shout: "Jesus is the way, the truth, and the light", or "life", depending on the translation. But I kind of like what Pilate said after he heard what Jesus had to say, "What is truth"? I like that Pilate was intrigued with the answers given by the Messiah. It left him wondering what the truth is.

Do you have courage to find out the truth? So far you're doing well. Keep reading and have the courage to ask for things to be revealed to you. In all of your studies, have the courage to ask the question: What is the Truth? Ask the Lord to reveal the Truth, not a man. He said the comforter will come, and he is here to answer all Truths. So...**ask**.

The Kingdom of God is to be proclaimed, not persuaded. The gospel is not delivered to man to persuade men of the deity of the Messiah, but it is to be proclaimed to mankind. The Messiah told his disciples to watch and pray. "Try the spirit by the spirit and see if it is of God" (1 John 4:1). This is a term used in the Bible to describe the process of spreading the gospel. When a man proclaims the gospel he is trying the spirit by the spirit of the company he keeps (among those in his presence). Therefore the Messiah stated to his disciples to "watch"-- see if the gospel resonates with the persons you are talking with. If not, wipe the dust of your feet and move on.

This is very important; you should bookmark this page. We have been misled in thinking that we should influence an individual to "accept the Messiah as your Lord and Savior". But you cannot accept the Messiah as Lord by merely saying the Lord's Prayer. How many times have you seen that on T.V.? You know what I mean, a T.V. minister says, "Repeat after me: I accept you as my Lord and Savior; now you are a born again; now sow a seed by calling the number below to send me some money." That's a lie. All lies. Stop it. They don't say what it actually means to have a lord over our entire life, neither to we take the time on our own to contemplate what that **really** means, or people wouldn't make that emotionally driven phone call after a 20 minute message. In that one moment can a person really decide to completely give themselves over to a power, ruler or authority? In that one moment does a person realize they will be surrendering to a deity that will now rule over their money, their time, their actions, their speech; should I go on? Should I mention that it is written that a person who does not give up everything cannot be his disciple? Everything. What's most likely happening is the short prayer followed by the promise of salvation is following a message about prosperity or a message where we have a better picture about the Messiah being our Savior, but definitely not our **Lord**. Save me and lord over me are two different things; two very different things that need to be deeply considered. What does the Messiah say about salvation? Well, when approached by Nicodemus about such accounts he said you must be born again, which is the baptism.

> Jesus answered and said unto him, **Verily, verily, I say unto thee, Except a man be born again, he cannot see the kingdom of God.**

> Jesus answered, **Verily, verily, I say unto thee, Except a man be born of water and [of] the Spirit, he cannot enter into the kingdom of God.**

That which is born of the flesh is flesh; and
that which is born of the Spirit is spirit.
(John 3:3, 5-6)

This is important, as the baptism is the acceptance into the Kingdom according to verse 5. It is the act of surrendering your spirit to God. You are voluntarily giving your soul back to God. Remember what is born of the flesh is flesh; and that which is born of Spirit is Spirit. This is the premise of Spiritual DNA.

We continue to hear people spouting the word love. "Jesus loves you!" It is obvious to the believer that the Messiah loves them, but recruiting every living soul walking the earth by saying that "Jesus" loves them and he came to bring them peace needs to stop. What did the Messiah say; not those letters from Paul; but what did the Messiah say? Did he come for peace? Well, let's read. He said he came to bear witness to the Truth, though many find it hard to agree. Nevertheless, he came to bring about an awakening among the Lost Sheep even if it divided a household where different strands of Spiritual DNA were found. The Messiah did not care if it broke up the home; he was only interested in regaining his Lost Sheep; at whatever cost. Read it for yourself:

> *Think not that I am come to send peace*
> *on earth: I came not to send peace, but a*
> *sword.*
>
> *For I am come to set a man at variance*
> *against his father, and the daughter*
> *against her mother, and the daughter in*
> *law against her mother in law.*
>
> *And a man's foes [shall be] they of his*
> *own household.*
>
> *He that loveth father or mother more than*
> *me is not worthy of me: and he that loveth*
> *son or daughter more than me is not*
> *worthy of me.*
>
> *And he that taketh not his cross, and*
> *followeth after me, is not worthy of me.*
> *(Matthew 10:34-38)*

Do you see how this works? If you were inducted into a clandestine organization like the CIA, KGB, or any prominent secret organization, it would be imperative that you forsake father, mother, sister and brother for that organization, along with your spouse and **your** beliefs or religion for that clandestine organization's agenda. If you can understand what is required of you and you then become a full-fledged agent vowing secrecy, then why would you question the writings of this book? Is what I am saying foreign to you? We are at **war**. Keep this in mind as you continue to read.

> *And there went great multitudes with him:*
> *and he turned, and said unto them,*
>
> **If any [man] come to me, and hate not his**
> **father, and mother, and wife, and**
> **children, and brethren, and sisters, yea,**
> **and his own life also, he cannot be my**
> **disciple.** *(Luke 14:25-26)*

Again, in the current sequence of events, the kingdoms continue to find themselves in confrontation, the surging back and forth of the troops, and the casualties of war.

In the passage below, the Messiah uses physical war as his analogy while making spiritual war more of a reality. Let's say you are a king, but the king you are going up against has twice as many men. Won't you first consider if you are able to even win this war? If you don't want to die and you don't to loose any of your men in battle, then there is only one way out. Prior to the troops invading your camp you would send a delegate, or delegates, to waive the white flag of peace. If you do not offer the proper terms, being that the opposing king is intelligent, he will not hesitate to demand **all** of your weapons, that **all** of your men be his men, and for **you** to now be subject to him. If you can't give up everything, including your kingship, then you are not ready to surrender and be one army with the opposing king and his army! Bottom line!

> *Or what king, going to make war against*
> *another king, sitteth not down first, and*
> *consulteth whether he be able with ten*
> *thousand to meet him that cometh*
> *against him with twenty thousand?*

Or else, while the other is yet a great way off, he sendeth an ambassage, and desireth conditions of peace.

So likewise, whosoever he be of you that forsaketh not all that he hath, he cannot be my disciple. (Luke 14:31-33)

The Messiah was speaking of war and requesting for repentance among the Lost Sheep. He acknowledges that the sheep should not have dual allegiance and should surrender all immediately and that he who cannot surrender all is not his disciple. Or when the war escalates, then the consideration for peace shall be withdrawn and the King of Kings shall commence with victory.

Remember what was written earlier about the Lost Sheep knowing his voice, or the Lost Sheep being God's children? Well, they have been his children from the beginning of time. Remember earlier where it's written that you cannot influence a person to become a part of the Kingdom, but only proclaim the gospel and see how it resonates like the Messiah did? Well it's true. Millions have been lied to about this, which may have to do with efforts to raise money. I don't know why, but it's a lie nonetheless. Who is a part of the Lost Sheep? It's already pre-ordained.

The fall of man, the prophecies regarding the Messiah, the birth of the Messiah , the gathering of the Lost Sheep, the death on the cross, the defeat of Satan, the day of Judgment, everything, I mean everything is pre-ordained: **even you.**

How long you will be lost, when you will have a spiritual awakening, how old you will become, how many children you will have, all of it is pre-ordained. Now isn't that something to choke down? Oh... Oh... Oh... I know, wait a minute. Let's review:

The fall of man, the prophecies regarding the Messiah, the birth of the Messiah , the gathering of the Lost Sheep, the death on the cross, the defeat of Satan, the day of Judgment, everything, I mean everything is pre-ordained: **but not you!** But not you?

See, if I wanted to lie to you like you have been lied to from the pulpit, then I would say everything is pre-ordained, but you are the only thing living that is not pre-ordained: you see, you have a choice. You have choices to make and it is my job to influence you on those choices while collecting money from you in tithes and offerings. Not!

Who you are, what you are, when you will stop being who and what you are, are all pre-ordained. It's just not good for business to tell such things to the masses. You see, if you are of the Lost Sheep, then you can hear his voice. Period. If you are not, then you will not submit to him. Remember this verse:

> **But seek ye first the kingdom of God, and his righteousness; and all these things shall be added unto you.** (Matthew 6:33)

The Messiah was referring to the Lost Sheep worrying about food, clothes, and other material items similar to the mindset of the Gentiles and was admonishing them "to seek first the Kingdom of God and his righteousness;" and all these things would be added to them, not for a person to choose the Kingdom of God, then God will give them all that they desire. Just "name it and claim it."

"Name it and claim it" is the biggest hoax known to man. It is unfair to promote such attainable blessings without a person being the Lost Sheep, or without the Messiah abiding in you and you abiding in him. It's a circus stunt used by ministers to work up the emotions of the masses. Look people: remember the truth works all the time. 1 + 1 = 2, whether you are angry, sad, happy or joyful, it will always equal 2 because this is the truth. "Name it and claim it" for the sake of claiming it does not work all the time.

Hey, you have read a small glimpse about the Kingdom of God. There is so much more for you to know. I will do my best to share with you the gospel and expose to you the church's view of the scriptures, what they want you to know, and how they continue to work hard to brain wash its members to follow them, the church and not the gospel. That's why more churches are becoming seminars with tape series after tape series.

The church and the Kingdom of God are not the same. It would have been nice if this were so, but it's not. We need to examine once more what the church really is and where it came from.

Evil ones exist. The Messiah stated over, and over, and over again in the book of John, Matthew, Mark and Luke that we are not alone. The evidence is overwhelming. Check out this passage and hear was the Messiah is saying:

> But he answered and said, **Every plant, which my heavenly Father hath not planted, shall be rooted up.**
>
> **Let them alone: they be blind leaders of the blind. And if the blind lead the blind, both shall fall into the ditch.** (Matthew 15:13-14)

He continues to urge his disciples to not be concerned with them. When you have a team leader at your church, pleading with you to go out and minister to the masses, remember what you have learned. Proclaim the gospel, see if it resonates, if not, leave them alone.

> **[Ye] hypocrites, well did Esaias prophesy of you, saying,**
>
> **This people draweth nigh unto me with their mouth, and honoureth me with [their] lips; but their heart is far from me.**
>
> **But in vain they do worship me, teaching [for] doctrines the commandments of men.**
> (Matthew 15:7-9)

In Matthew 15:7-9 you have those who worship the Messiah with their mouth and honor him with their lips, but their heart is far from him. For the most part, when the Messiah spoke of the heart he was referring to Spiritual DNA, the character of man, which is often misunderstood or deliberately improperly taught by the church. It continues to propagate untruths concerning who the Jews are, untruths regarding the gospel of the Kingdom, untruths to the poor, swindling them out of money continually. It's not about the church. It's about the Lord. Do you think I'm being hard on the church? Well listen to what the Lord had to say according to Jeremiah:

> *Thus saith the LORD of hosts, Hearken not*
> *unto the words of the prophets that*
> *prophesy unto you: they make you vain:*
> *they speak a vision of their own heart,*
> *[and] not out of the mouth of the LORD.*
> *They say still unto them that despise me,*
> *The LORD hath said, Ye shall have peace;*
> *and they say unto every one that walketh*
> *after the imagination of his own heart, No*
> *evil shall come upon you. (Jeremiah*
> *23:16-17)*

No evil shall come upon you? (Laugh out loud) Whatever! How often do you hear that coming from the pulpit as a minister is telling the crowd what it wants to hear, which is often about health or wealth? "If you'll just sow 66 dollars; the Lord told me to tell you to pick up the phone; some of you can sow $1,000.00 now." It needs to stop people!

Hey let's finish what Jeremiah was saying. Hypocrites will lie on God continually because the masses don't, or won't, read for themselves. The church has been misleading the masses since its beginnings, which were initiated by leaders in Catholicism. Let's continue to read:

> *For who hath stood in the counsel of the*
> *LORD, and hath perceived and heard his*
> *word? who hath marked his word, and*
> *heard [it]?*
>
> *Behold, a whirlwind of the LORD is gone*
> *forth in fury, even a grievous whirlwind: it*
> *shall fall grievously upon the head of the*
> *wicked.*
>
> *The anger of the LORD shall not return,*
> *until he have executed, and till he have*
> *performed the thoughts of his heart: in the*
> *latter days ye shall consider it perfectly.*
> *(Jeremiah 27:18-20)*

God is saying that whatever he says will happen, will happen. Period. If it didn't happen, God said he didn't say it.

I have not sent these prophets, yet they ran: I have not spoken to them, yet they prophesied.

But if they had stood in my counsel, and had caused my people to hear my words, then they should have turned them from their evil way, and from the evil of their doings.

[Am] I a God at hand, saith the LORD, and not a God afar off?

Can any hide himself in secret places that I shall not see him? saith the LORD. Do not I fill heaven and earth? saith the LORD.

I have heard what the prophets said, that prophesy lies in my name, saying, I have dreamed, I have dreamed.

How long shall [this] be in the heart of the prophets that prophesy lies? yea, [they are] prophets of the deceit of their own heart;

Which think to cause my people to forget my name by their dreams which they tell every man to his neighbour, as their fathers have forgotten my name for Baal.

The prophet that hath a dream, let him tell a dream; and he that hath my word, let him speak my word faithfully. What [is] the chaff to the wheat? saith the LORD.

[Is] not my word like as a fire? saith the LORD; and like a hammer [that] breaketh the rock in pieces?

Therefore, behold, I [am] against the prophets, saith the LORD, that steal my words every one from his neighbour.

Behold, I [am] against the prophets, saith the LORD, that use their tongues, and say, He saith

Behold, I [am] against them that prophesy false dreams, saith the LORD, and do tell them, and cause my people to err by their lies, and by their lightness; yet I sent them not, nor commanded

*them: therefore they shall not profit this
people at all, saith the LORD. (Jeremiah
23:21-32)*

Whew, that was a lot to read, but very necessary. These prophets shall not profit this people at all, said the Lord. Hey--do you really want empirical data on why the church is not the Kingdom of God? Well, let's examine.

We covered the existence of things as it relates to factual realms, or should I say "geometric plains" for the intellectually endowed, but kingdoms nonetheless. Let's get back to the relationship between man and the bigger picture. When we examine the church, we have to start with the supposed primary nature of why it exists, and that would be to transcend. For many, it's for man to transcend through a vehicle such as religion and find himself in a higher plane of existence. In religion, **transcendence** is a condition or state of being that surpasses physical existence. It is affirmed in the concept of the divine in the major religious traditions and contrasts with the notion of God as a higher state of existence to strive for.

If you are a part of the Christian church you are most likely subscribing the transcendence application. You are also following 90% of the Catholic order. If you fall under Protestant, Baptist, Lutheran, apostolic, non-denominational designations, and so on, then you are working toward transcendence. No matter what your denomination or non-denomination is, you are still functioning as "Catholic under protest". You're working hard to transcend from being a sinner to a saint. You don't think so? Well, let's look at the Catholic.

Catholic [**kath**-uh-lik, **kath**-lik] Origin: 1300–1350; ME < L *catholicus* < Gk *katholikós* general, equiv. to *kathól(ou)* **universally** (contr. of phrase *katà hólou* **according to the whole.**)

According to the whole? Even though the mainstream church had been operational since about 40 AD, the mainstream church finally changed its name to Catholic. How many times have you heard that there is a church and a universal church? Remember that one? Ministers propagated and replaced the universal church in front of the masses and discarded the Kingdom? You see, the Kingdom is not the universal church. The Catholic Church is the universal church. So why is this conveyed to the masses?

Inclusion, that's why. How else do you graft in the "right to a covenant" that was given to the Hebrews? How could the majority of Gentiles and any who are not of the Lost Sheep participate in this new religion called Christianity? This was a great way to control the masses through religion. Remember earlier in this book when we examined the authenticity of who the true Hebrews were and the difference with the Greeks who call themselves Jews today? Remember Hellenistic occurrences in Chapter 2?

The Greeks! Well, the same Greeks who took over Israel and Egypt and stole the legacies of the original Semitic people in that region also disregarded the true followers of the Messiah, calling them and their writings heresy. They converted what they felt should be propagated into a religion to control the masses. The Greek-Romans or Greco Romans are more commonly known as the Byzantine Empire and are responsible for this.

The **Byzantine Empire** or **Byzantium** is the term conventionally used since the 19th century to describe the Greek-speaking Roman Empire of the Middle Ages, and was centered on its capital of Constantinople. During much of its history, it was known to many of its Western contemporaries as the **Empire of the Greeks** because of the dominance of Greek language, culture and population. (King dominance versus Greek dominance.)

Well along with the Greco kingdoms came its Greco gods. By combining the paganism of the Greeks, the rituals of the Hebrews, and the testimonies of the followers of the Messiah, you can put together a religion and call it Christianity.

Kingdom of God	American Church	Catholicism
According to biblical writings the Sabbath on Saturday	Sabbath on Sunday	Sabbath on Sunday
Commune with the Spirit	Communion	Communion
According to biblical writings Full emersion baptism, According to People of the Way spiritual baptism (Tongues)	Full emersion baptism	Sprinkling of water
Confession to God of your desire to become pure	Confession of sins to God	Confession of sins to a priest
Scriptures can be understood by normal people	Scriptures need interpretation by minister not by the people	Scriptures cannot be understood by normal people, but the priest
The truth of the kingdom, the baptism and being of the Lost Sheep bring you to an awakening	Accepting Jesus as your Lord and Savior is the way to salvation	The Bible plus traditions are needed to find salvation
The Rock in scripture referred to the philosopher's stone	Jesus is the rock	Peter is the rock
According to biblical writings The Messiah is head of the Kingdom	Jesus is head of the church	The Pope is head of the church
According to biblical writings Mary had more children than just the Messiah	Mary had more children than just the Messiah	**Mary had no other children; a perpetual Virgin.**

Many more differences exist, but did you notice how the Sabbath was converted to Sunday, fusing the worship of the sun god with the worship of Elohim? At any rate, the list is extensive. You see these Roman Catholics assembled what they felt should be taught to the masses, and called it the **Received Text** (also known as Canon #85).

The Roman Catholics or Greco Catholics or just plainly, the church, has ordained a man to stand in place of God on Earth. They call him the Pope (which means Father). Catholics believe the pope to be the Vicar of Christ. In the broadest sense, a **vicar** (from the Latin *vicarius*) is anyone acting "in the person of" or agent for a superior (compare "vicarious")for which the Pope is held in esteem, while the other faith communities refuse to acknowledge Petrine Primacy among the bishops. Nevertheless, the office of the pope is called the "papacy".

This title of "the papacy" implies his supremacy and universal primacy, both of honor and jurisdiction, over the Catholic Church. Roman Catholics find justification for this in the words of the Messiah to St. Peter, "Feed my lambs...Feed my sheep" (John 21:15-17). The Catholic Church believes Jesus made St. Peter the leader of the Apostles, hence, Prince of the Apostles, which constituted him as the guardian of his entire flock (the Church) in his own place, thus making him his **Vicar** and fulfilling the promise he made in Matthew 16:18-19.

You must pay close attention. You see, since Satan is coming with such wrath as stated in Revelation, why wouldn't he just take over the kingdom movement by establishing his own version of the truth and call it Christianity? Why not use his influence and energy to focus the salvation of the Lost Sheep on the papacy and not on the gospel or even the papacy under protest which is what we have among the American churches today?

Why is it that 85% of what is taught in the church today consists of the Pauline letters, Romans, Corinthians, Galatians, Thessalonians and so on? Why are the Greco's, after infiltrating nation after nation, taking them over from within one after another while running their secret societies, still Hellenizing to this day? Hmmmm. Yet all of these clandestine operations present themselves as solutions to Satan's continued attempt to destroy Man, the Lost Sheep in particular.

Hey people this has been going on since the beginning of man. In Genesis 3 God speaks of the war between the children of man and the children of Satan.

> And I will put enmity between thee and
> the woman, and between thy seed and
> her seed; it shall bruise thy head, and
> thou shalt bruise his heel. (Genesis 3:15)

He continues in Revelation 12:

> And the dragon was wroth with the
> woman, and went to make war with the
> remnant of her seed, which keep the

> commandments of God, and have the
> testimony of Jesus Christ. (Revelations
> 12:17)

War among the seeds-- those which keep the commandments of God--Can you say Spiritual DNA?

The Church; the Kingdom; the Kingdom vs. the Church. Oh I can hear it now, "Brother that can't be true, the Bible says this about the church, the Bible says that about the church". No, Paul said this about the church; Paul said that about the church. But what did the Messiah say?

> **And I say also unto thee, That thou art
> Peter, and upon this rock I will build my
> church; and the gates of hell shall not
> prevail against it.** (Matthew 16:18)

> **And if he shall neglect to hear them, tell
> [it] unto the church: but if he neglect to
> hear the church, let him be unto thee as
> an heathen man and a publican**
> (Matthew 18:17)

And, if you are interested in what Paul said about to whom the church belongs, or who the "vicar" is:

> According to the grace of God which is
> given unto me, as a wise masterbuilder, I
> have laid the foundation, and another
> buildeth thereon. But let every man take
> heed how he buildeth thereupon.

> For other foundation can no man lay than
> that is laid, which is Jesus Christ. (1
> Corinthians 3:10-11)

Did Paul know the Messiah was the **only** foundation? Not Mary, not Peter, not money. If you lay a foundation other than the Messiah, then what? Paul continues:

*For it hath been declared unto me of you,
my brethren, by them [which are of the
house] of Chloe, that there are
contentions among you.*

*Now this I say, that every one of you saith,
I am of Paul; and I of Apollos; and I of
Cephas; and I of Christ.*

*Is Christ divided? was Paul crucified for
you? or were ye baptized in the name of
Paul?*
(1 Corinthians 1:11-13)

Maybe when Paul wrote the above words he did not expect that other words in his letters to people and churches would someday overshadow the words of the Messiah. According to the King James Version (also known as Canon #85), outside of the Messiah addressing the churches in Revelation, he only stated the word church three times and the word Kingdom approximately 159 times. Woe, what tangled webs we weave.

The term *church* (Anglo-Saxon, *cirice, circe*; Modern German, **Kirche**; Sw., *Kyrka*) is the name employed in the Teutonic languages to render the Greek *ekklesia* (*ecclesia*). The derivation of the word has been much debated. It is now agreed that it is derived from the Greek *kyriakon* (*cyriacon*), i.e. the Lord's house, a term which from the third century used, as well as *ekklesia*, to signify a Christian place of worship.

So church is an Anglo-Saxon word from Europe not from Africa, or the Middle East where the Hebrew and Semitic languages come from; it's really not Aramaic, but an English word translated from the Greek word ekklesia. Didn't the Messiah speak Aramaic? So what did he really say in those two verses in Matthew?

He spoke Aramaic and he said
qahal 'êdah which meant the
gathering, the communion of the
disciples and the Lost Sheep that
were beginning to awaken among
the masses within the early

73

communions. Hence, the word community means a social, religious, or other group sharing common characteristics or interests and perceived or perceiving itself as distinct in some respect from the larger society within which it exists. So if you translate it from the Hebrew which is similar to Aramaic into English you would get:

> **And I say also unto thee, That thou art Peter, and upon this rock I will build my community; and the gates of hell shall not prevail against it.** *(Matthew 16:18)*

> **And if he shall neglect to hear them, tell [it] unto the community: but if he neglect to hear the community, let him be unto thee as an heathen man and a publican** *(Matthew 18:17)*

How many times have you heard that the early church lived in communes, or communities? They gathered all of their goods and money together; they sold property; they put all their money together and used it to feed their group, the community within. In real estate law, there are different measures of ownership. When you receive a grant deed to real estate it is durably noted whether you own it in sovereignty, which means by yourself--answering to no one, or if it's community property, known as tenants in common. The necessity of this notation in real estate is that you cannot differentiate where one of the owners' ownership begins and ends from another owners' ownership. Everyone owns it all together.

The church today has been fully exposed to the fact that early Christians lived in communes and they communicated from one community to another. These communities were often underground in nature. Hence Paul's letters were able to make it to the community for which he intended, in spite of his incarceration.

Unlike the Kingdom of God being represented by the communes and true followers, the church has continued to work hard at suppressing the Truth. It and the angel that leads it, the fallen angel that is, is about the destruction of Man and the destruction of the Lost Sheep.
You see the best way to win a war is to cut your enemy off at the pass, control bridges, highways

74

and byways, impose sanctions and embargos, and usurp the connection between the sheep and its shepherd by intercepting and controlling accessibility and calling your interception a name similar to enemy or in this case: **Christianity**.

It's that simple: have the sheep focus on the epistles (letters) and not the gospel; suppress the authority of women; suppress who can become a priest based on ethnos; and receive heavy influence of the cosmos, Wicca, astrology, and the institution of pantheism in place; making false proclamations of supremacy by your holiness the Pope, and suffering all dominion and church authority to the Pope, not the Messiah.

The Catholic Church is very clandestine. When a Pope dies, the Cardinals perform a secret ritual that is used to pick the next Pope. Arrangements are made with the **Camerlengo** to pick the next person to be incarnated with the **spirit of the Papacy**. After choosing three assistant Cardinals, the Camerlengo will call a Conclave which will meet in the Sistine Chapel. The Conclave will consist of 120 Cardinal electors and takes its name from the Latin words "cum clave" -- "with a key." This gathering is thus called because it is conducted under the utmost secrecy, the Cardinals at one time being literally locked into the Sistine Chapel where the voting takes place, until they came to a decision.

The election process must begin between 15 and 20 days after the death. Upon entering the Conclave, the Cardinals swear an oath of secrecy. The penalty for breaking secrecy is automatic excommunication. The secrecy of the Conclave is taken so seriously that the Cardinals cannot communicate with anyone in the outside world as it goes on--even windows are painted over so they can't see out, nor can anyone see in. Newspapers, television, radio--all are forbidden.

Then there is the American church under protest. You still may not agree that American Christianity is not connected to Catholicism, but Christians are reading a book deemed holy by Catholics not by God. The Pope deemed the 66 books as holy to control the masses, but left out many writings that are worthy of your research and labeled them heretical, which include many 1st century writings, or apologetics.

Everyone who is Greek is not evil nor is everyone that attends a Catholic mass or service. Many of these people are from Hellenized countries and governments and thus controlled from within. America is not excluded. The Masonic ranks and their rituals are incorporated in much of the architecture in Washington D.C. Many Capitol buildings around the U.S. were designed with paranormal "infusion". The Pentagon, the Washington Monument and the Greek Goddess Libertis, who towers over the shore of N.Y. holding the torch of the illuminated ones, are all demonstrations of this "infusion". Statue of Liberty, right? I don't think so!

If a nation says it is mostly Christian, then why does its money display symbols and designations attributable to the black arts, sacred geometry, symbols from the watchers and Egyptian Hieroglyphs? Make no mistake, the Greco's are everywhere: in America, the Vatican, Israel, the United Kingdom, and more. The Greco's have infiltrated these governments and they are working hard to destroy Man.

We are not fighting against flesh and blood, but powers and might's. Do you think that they are not connected? I dare you to throw a rock at Israel, let alone throw a boulder, and you will see American jets and American missiles coming your way. (This just in: In April 2008 while Sen. Hillary Clinton was campaigning for President of the U.S. many news programs and newspapers have quoted the Senator as saying we will attack Iran if Iran attacks Israel.)

Isn't that amazing? You will have multi-million dollar jets and missiles coming your way. What does Israel do for America that warrants such protection? No other country in the world has ever received this kind of protection from America. Mind you, Israel and the American CIA both flew in individuals who were promised by God in the Abrahamic covenant, that is to say, real Hebrews, not the Greco government of Israel. God made a covenant with the real Jews, not the synagogues of Satan.

Do you still think Christianity is not connected to Catholicism? America turned its sword on itself, and blamed another for doing so and lied to the masses in order to advance closer to achieving this "new world order". Wage a war against Iraq under false pretenses and what did America do on the first day of arrival in Baghdad? She went directly for the goods that motivated the invasion of Iraq, or war on Iraq, in the first place.

Blood for oil? I don't think so. Religious artifacts be the booty that this pirate was seeking. As recorded a "Grand Theft of Antiquities" took place in the National Museum of Iraq (U.S. Tank in the door guarding against unwanted guests shown above.) between the 8th and 12th of April 2003, when some staff returning to the building noticed the items missing. U.S. forces, headed by Marine Col. Matthew Bogdanos, entered the compound on April 16th and initiated an investigation on the 21st of the same month. His investigation indicated that despite claims to the contrary, no U.S. forces had looted the building and that there were three separate thefts by three distinct groups over the four days.

On May 7, 2003, U.S. officials announced that nearly 40,000 manuscripts and 700 artifacts belonging to the National Museum of Iraq in Baghdad were **recovered by U.S. Customs agents working with museum experts in Iraq**. Some looters had returned items after promises of rewards and amnesty, and many items previously reported missing had actually been hidden in secret storage vaults at the museum prior to the outbreak of war.

No, U.S. forces had not looted the building for religious artifacts. Hmmmm. Then how did the robbers know of the secret storage vaults? How did they know where on the wall to push to open the secret door? Isn't it amazing that if you create enough confusion and misplace enough items, then once certain items start showing up, well, shall we say, at U.S. Customs, that the masses will not be able to distinguish any criminal or suspicious motivation or foul play? First rule of thumb in committing homicide or murder: kill your subject;

ransack the house to make it look like a home invasion or robbery, throwing the detectives off of your true intent and your scent.

Hey, I am an American and I love my country, but it's not my country that's doing this, it's the evil ones, those with bad Spiritual DNA in the likeness of human bodies. The seed of Satan is the perpetrator: this evil seed is all around us. White, Black, Asian, Hispanics, Israelites, English, Canadians, Irish. It does not discriminate against flesh, for the spirit of Man is what it is after.

They are among us. Each day you turn on the news, you see the results of their recent attempts at Hellenization.

The American church continues to assist the Greco's by propagating lies about salvation and how you can or cannot be saved. The Kingdom of God is not preached and the misinterpretation of the Scriptures continues. The parts of the King James Bible that are in fact the Scriptures are used along with other writings to amass cash for the church. The modern European version of Believers does not operate like 1st century Believers, like communes. The First Century Believers were empowered. The European church lacks power.

If you took one of the elements out of water, then you would not have the substance water. Try it. Take **H**ydrogen out of the formula for water. I bet you'll die of thirst since inhaling oxygen is not the same as drinking water. Likewise many Christians are perishing for the lack of knowledge. When you take **H**ydrogen out of H_2O you're doing the same thing. Change communion into church; tell individuals to pray, but take fasting out of the Bible; preach that tongues are not for today; teach that full emersion water baptism is not necessary, but just sprinkling something on you is enough. Many practices have merely become traditions that lack power. Well let's just say that Satan has been making progress in his advancement against the Kingdom of God. But Satan, you are a liar. We will no longer allow traditional beliefs to overshadow historical facts.

Let me ask you something: what is a con man's greatest asset and how does he used it to lure his victim into allowing him to swindle something from them? He gets them to believe in him. He works hard to discourage the victim from trying to know and understand what he's doing because knowledge is power. He works hard to keep them out of the knowing, and get them into the believing. Well, once the con man achieves this, the rest is history.

Stop believing in God. Take time out and **get to know God**. Love God because you got to know him. Stop believing, my friends. A belief is an exercise expended due to the lack of knowing. When you cannot substantiate a subject matter, you can only resort to believing it. Detrimentally, belief can be so powerful, that when Truth stares us in the face we choose to hold on to belief for dear life. When the bricks of historical fact are stacked against our traditional beliefs, our minds and hearts can be so attached to the illusion that we find it easier to protect and defend the plan of Satan's slow deception instead of abandoning it and wrestling with the fact that we've been bamboozled.

Again, stop believing; know that God. Stop believing that Canon #85, which was put together by the Pope and authorized by King James, is infallible and that all and every page is true. Read it, there are intentional insertions of misrepresentation in it. Study it for yourself so that you can rightly divide the word of Truth. Know what King of Kings is and understand what that means.

Next you will get the closest look ever at what Spiritual DNA is all about as we deal with the **Church Under Siege:** Assemblies of GOD, Illuminati, Pimps in the Pulpit, the Era of Name it and Claim it, and most of all In the Name of...

THE CHURCH UNDER SIEGE
Chapter 4

This chapter, "The Church Under Siege", is about the Lost Sheep that are being led astray by false shepherds. The Lost Sheep go beyond the true Children of Israel back to the beginning of the Fall of Man. Currently; the Kingdom of God is suffering at the hand of the evil ones although the Messiah's atonement was for the reconciliation of the Kingdom. The Messiah petitioned God to allow the Lost Sheep to be exonerated from such current and future experiences with the evil ones by speaking specifically with God about the apostles and the Lost
Sheep, which as many of you all ready know, are the "chosen children" of the Kingdom of God and its spiritual descendants who are still here. Read it for yourself:

I pray not that thou shouldest take them out of the world, but that thou shouldest keep them from the evil.

They are not of the world, even as I am not of the world.

Sanctify them through thy truth: thy word is truth.

As thou hast sent me into the world, even so have I also sent them into the world. And for their sakes I sanctify myself, that they also might be sanctified through the truth. Neither pray I for these alone, but for them also which shall believe on me through their word; (John 17:15-20)

The Messiah continues to differentiate between the Spiritual DNA of the Lost Sheep (including the Apostles) and of the evil ones. The Spirit within The Messiah is the same that inhabits the Lost Sheep. He speaks about Believers being those who believe because of their Spiritual DNA and not because of their choosing of the mind. You don't think so? Well, read this:

Ye have not chosen me, but I have chosen you, and ordained you, that ye should go and bring forth fruit, and [that] your fruit should remain: that whatsoever ye shall ask of the Father in my name, he may give it you. (John 15:16)

The Messiah is talking with his disciples about their being pre-ordained and pre-chosen for such a time as this. It kills me how people speak against things that are pre-ordained or even against some of the Calvinistic viewpoint. The European Church (or I'm sorry the American Church) continues to try to strip the relationship between the Lost Sheep and the Lord with such falsehood. I guess that in order to make the masses continue to believe that they need the church structure in order to be with God, that is to say, "Let me help influence you in the fact that you need us to help you to choose the Lord". Hmmmmm. Why do I need the church to help me find the Lord? The church is part of Satan's Kingdom, controlled, censured, manipulated, and propagated by the leaders of the church movement. It has nothing to do with the Kingdom of God that the Messiah speaks of. Let's continue with the writing of John. The Messiah continues to talk to his apostles in John 15:

If ye were of the world, the world would
love his own: but because ye are not of
the world, but I have chosen you out of
the world, therefore the world hateth you.
(John 15:19)

The church continues to lie to the masses about what is in the world versus what is sanctified and try to sell the fact that they can be secular at 9:00 am and by 9:15am the same day, be sanctified only to return to secular thoughts and actions by 10:00am that same morning.
Stop it people.

Do these comments offend you? This study is not about criticizing a person's religious views, but about finding out the Truth and knowing the methods used by Satan. So let's continue to explore. Come on a journey with me for a moment. Let's use the purity of animals to explain this: According to Matthew Chapter 13, purebred dogs have been mixed with other crossbreed dogs and have created more mixed breeds or mutts. Now the Messiah comes to save the purebred dogs because through his divine knowledge he concluded that the continued mixing of these breeds will result in deformity, disease and death. The Messiah designs a whistle that only the purest breeds can hear and even some that are not as tainted through mixed breeding. He gathers a group of dogs and anoints them with the ability to whistle this very high pitch. The Messiah then tells them, "Go through out the world and blow your special whistle, if any dogs hear you and come running, bless them, baptize them back into the kingdom, and let them know that their salvation is at hand. Tell them to come out from among the other dogs and be separate. Remember my faithful canines, these dogs are not choosing me, I am choosing them. Also there will be dogs that can't here this whistle, leave them. They are blind guides. They can't hear the whistle because they are not of us. Now go. I will return quickly to gather the pack of purebred dogs."

Far fetched? Not quite. What if, in John 3:16, God so loved his pure breeds that he gave his only begotten son a whistle? That whosoever should hear the whistle would not perish but have everlasting life. Would that be easier to understand?

Referencing John 15:19, If you were of a mutt breed that breed would love you, but since you are not, you are chosen out of all the world of all breeds and those breeds hated you.

What about 2 Corinthians 6:14-17:

> *Be ye not unequally yoked together with unbelievers: for what fellowship hath righteousness with unrighteousness? and what communion hath light with darkness?*
>
> *And what concord hath Christ with Belial? or what part hath he that believeth with an infidel?*
>
> *And what agreement hath the temple of God with idols? For ye are the temple of the living God; as God hath said, I will dwell in them, and walk in [them]; and I will be their God, and they shall be my people.*
>
> *Wherefore come out from among them, and be ye separate, saith the Lord, and touch not the unclean [thing]; and I will receive you...*
> *(2 Corinthians 6:14-17)*

The Church constantly contradicts itself on these verses. The Church programs its members to not fellowship with unbelievers and by the same token, to go out and persuade unbelievers to believe. Show them love. Put your best foot forward. Hey, we have books on how to witness.
How to witness? What kind of malarkey is that! According to Mark 1 the Messiah said "...Come ye after me, and I will make you to become fishers of men." So where exactly does the "how-to" book come in if it is the Messiah who makes someone a witness? The Scriptures above were referring to the Lost Sheep versus the evil ones.

Do you see why the gospel cannot be influenced? Just proclaimed and studied. That's it. Study the word, and the rest will be taught by "the Comforter" the Messiah said would come. The Comforter is here people, oh it's here. The evidence of what is being said in this book is overwhelming, and at the risk of being redundant, I have held back a floodgate of scripture to prove this point.

Now what you, my assistant, have been waiting for, is the truth about the American Church, or shall I say the "church under protest". In case you don't remember what the "church under protest" means: it's individuals who study Canon #85 that was put together by the Catholic Church and belong to sects of individuals who, having left some but not all, but some of the rituals and beliefs of the Catholic Church and branched themselves into their own sects like, Lutheran, Pentecostal, Baptist, Later Day Saints, and let us not leave out the non-denominationalists.

Many of these sects fall under the fraternity known as The Assemblies of God, which has its roots in a religious revival that began in the late 1800's and swept into the 20th century with widespread repetition of biblical spiritual experiences, according to their founders and its dogma, went throughout the U.S. and abroad.

According to the Assemblies of God, at the time of inception, many Christians in the United States and other parts of the world began to feel a need for more of God's power operating in their lives. Individually and in groups, they began to earnestly pray and seek to conform their commitments and experiences in to what they believed was the New Testament pattern.

Now mind you, the Assemblies of God admits that there was and is a lack of power in the movement of the Spirit and in their studies. They associate the beginning of the modern Pentecostal revival to be generally traced to a prayer meeting at Bethel Bible College in Topeka, Kansas, on January 1, 1901. While many others had spoken in tongues previously during almost every period of spiritual revival, the recipients of the experience came through study of the Scriptures, and people thus came to believe that speaking in tongues is the biblical evidence for the baptism in the Holy Spirit. **This organization has thousands of organizations under its thumb, millions of church members.**

Can you say theocracy? I think so. The Assemblies of God have phenomenal influence over what goes on television, radio and what is disseminated among the masses as it relates to the Gospel. They greatly censor the material and have stripped ministers from their organization if that minister strays from their desired information for the masses. Hey ask Jimmy Swaggart, Carlton Person, Jim and Tammy Faye Baker and many more. This organization will impose their measured sanctions on anyone they can. If you are not a member, they will threaten television and radio stations with the financial consequences of continuing to carry your message on the network's stations like they did with the media over Dr. Fred K. Price.

Don't let the smiles fool you. An organization that big has clandestine sects within them and hidden agendas that can be felt, but rarely seen. I would not be surprised if they launched their own anti- "He that has an Ear" book campaign, like they did against the DaVinci Code. Now I don't agree with everything that the DaVinci Code said, Oh no, but the author has a right to say it.

After all, this is America, isn't it? Well, isn't it? I guess it depends on who you ask, but this theocracy is very powerful and some call the members of this organization "The Religious Right". You hear that a lot among the Republican Party: how the Assemblies of God looks sternly at the political party that swears it will uphold the mandates of this theocracy controlled by the Assemblies of God or WWC. "We the Republican Party will not sway from the unchangeable, uncompromising, views of what is **'right'**. We will not be Liberal in our accountings." You wonder why they have such disdain for what they call liberal Democrats? "Those liberals, roarrrrrrr!" How many times have you heard that?

The Greco's are everywhere, my friend. The Assemblies of God and its conservative views are shared by its co-membership of American Christians who invoke their more militant side while keeping the "clandestine" values on the primary circuit. I would not be surprised by how many members are actually parts of another religious sect called The Ku Klux Klan.

Ku Klux Klan (**KKK**) is the name of several past and present organizations in the United States that have advocated white supremacy, anti-Semitism, anti-Catholicism, racism, homophobia, anti-Communism and nativism. These organizations have often used terrorism, violence, and acts of

85

intimidation, such as cross burning and lynching, to oppress African Americans and other social or ethnic groups.

The Klan's first incarnation was in 1866. Founded by veterans of the Confederate Army, its main purpose was to resist Reconstruction, and it focused as much on intimidating "carpetbaggers" and "scalawags" as on putting down the freed slaves. The KKK quickly adopted violent methods. A rapid reaction set in, with the Klan's leadership disowning violence and Southern elites seeing the Klan as an excuse for federal troops to continue their activities in the South. The organization was in decline from 1868 to 1870 and was destroyed in the early 1870s by President Ulysses S. Grant's vigorous action under the Civil Rights Act of 1871 (also known as the Ku Klux Klan Act).

The second Ku Klux Klan rose to great prominence and spread from the South into the Midwest and Northern states and even into Canada. At its peak, Klan membership exceeded 4 million and comprised 20% of the adult white male population in many broad geographic regions, as high as 40% in some areas. Most of the membership resided in Midwestern states.

Through sympathetic elected officials, the KKK controlled the governments of Tennessee, Indiana, Oklahoma, and Oregon, in addition to some of the Southern legislatures. Klan influence was particularly strong in Indiana, where Republican Klansman Edward Jackson was elected governor in 1924, and the entire apparatus of state government was riddled with Klansmen. In another well-known example from the same year, the Klan decided to make **Anaheim, California**, into a model Klan city; it secretly took over the city council but was voted out in a special recall election.

The Klan and all its majestic order: let's see, what do they call the top dog in the Klan? Oh I remember, **The Grand Wizard**, or is it the Imperial **Wizard**? No? No, I know: it's the **Grand Dragon**. You see, at the start of the 20th Century, the KKK sprung up again as the Knights of the Ku Klux Klan. Still commonly referred to as the KKK, this incarnation has used a different system of titles for their officers. As you may have heard, the highest-ranking leaders of the modern Klan factions have more commonly used the title of Imperial Wizard. The title of Grand Wizard (or **Grand Dragon**, a common variation) now typically applies to the main KKK officer at a state or regional level.

Grand Dragon, Where did I hear the name Dragon? It sounds so familiar.

It's amazing how President Bush's "War on Terror" hasn't knocked on the door of this Grand Dragon nor has it snatched him from his underground hiding place and executed him. I guess he is too busy looking over the ocean at Israel bracing for any thrown rocks. What ever the case, he says he is not interested in homegrown terrorists. What was it that the Messiah said about such accounting? Oh yeah: **"A house divided would not stand".** I think that's what it was. But the Presidency is another story. The KKK believes strongly in what is written in Matthew, Chapter 13. They know that everyone that walks this earth is not of God, but many of their participants are misdirected into thinking that it has to do with skin color. Again, not true since we now know that it is Spiritual DNA that separates us from the evil ones. It's a slight of hand used by the Leaders of the KKK to promote Christian identity. Go look up Christian Identity. The Church finds itself propagating unlimited measures of pain to the Lost Sheep in many ways. You'll find so many atrocities performed "in the name of...."

Oh - don't forget the mind control mechanisms by the Pimps in the pulpit. *Oh yeah, we have Pimps in the pulpit-- real live ones, and undercover ones,* yet I don't know which one is worse. I think the undercover ones are. It's bad when you're being pimped by a minister without even knowing it. Some ministers are personally offended, all the while claiming "in the name of..." You see, if you miss church or tithe, go to a new church, etc., it means one less body and one less dollar that may take other bodies and other dollars with it. I challenge you to not be offended by the colorful way things are being said, and the fact remains that truth lies within these covers... but pay attention. There are pimps in the pulpit. Some actually peddle sex. (Not all, but some. And although there are some who do, we'll just focus on the others.) You know who I'm talking about - those pinky-ring wearing pimps in the pulpit.

In my opinion, there will be a special place in hell for them. A true hotspot with Players Ball arched over the doorway. I'm not being harsh; I have done the research and unfortunately found that women actually provide their money and bodies to ministers to do with as they please. Some in turn are able to be treasurers, or on the board of deacons and deaconesses, or probably the future first lady of the church.

87

The Greco's are so infiltrated within the walls of the church. They pimp products, not merely sex, but products consisting of countless numbers of tape series like Breaking out of Bondage, How to Pray in More Money, the Secrets of the Prayer Cloths, and hundreds of feel good books. Oh man, come on! What about the **Kingdom**? Tell the sheep about the **Kingdom**! These ministers will sell their own mother a tape on "how to have an effective prayer". No, No, No...don't you cut another tape or say another word without finding out the truth.

Stop lying to the masses. I have sparingly received good counsel from some of these tapes, but there's a place for that kind of counsel. Hey you can share some tapes on the psychology of how to act holy, but every sermon? It's called bait and switch. The members come for the life changing gospel, you promote that you are giving the life changing gospel revival and then switch up on the crowd, on how to receive a blessing from God - if you give a special offering that is. God chose us remember? He will bless and have mercy on whom he chooses, not if you do this..., or if you do that...! Come to *&^ revival, or Come to our Women's *&^%^%-- all of these conferences, year in and year out while the Lost Sheep just get more and more disenchanted and eventually, they stop coming to church. They can't put their finger on why. But something, well something, ahhhhh, I don't know, it just ain't right. They are not hearing the uncut words of God plain and simple. We can't have relationships with God through other people or what others say. We do have a direct connection to God. And what we are told is the gospel is not even being preached nor proclaimed to the masses. Remember what the Messiah did and said?

> And Jesus went about all Galilee, teaching in their synagogues, and **preaching the gospel of the kingdom**, and healing all manner of sickness and all manner of disease among the people. Matthew 4:23

> And Jesus went about all the cities and villages, teaching in their synagogues, and **preaching the gospel of the kingdom**, and healing every sickness and every disease among the people. Matthew 9:35

> And this **gospel of the kingdom shall be preached** in all the world for a witness unto all nations; and then shall the end come. Matthew 24:14

Now after that John was put in prison, Jesus came into Galilee, **preaching the gospel of the kingdom of God***, And saying, The time is fulfilled, and the* **kingdom** *of God is at hand: repent ye, and believe the* **gospel***. Mark 1:14-15*

It's overwhelming. The Messiah preached the Gospel. Preaching means to project your views onto another; to throw your thoughts outwardly toward someone; to propel, or proclaim.

Too many people are dying left and right behind such atrocities plagued by the church. What is propagated among the churches is not exclusive to Christianity. The views of controlling another "by the authority of…" or "in the name of…", is ramped. In the name of… is responsible for more deaths than any disease known to man.

In the name of …will cause a man to starve himself to death. It will influence a man to strap a bomb to his chest and walk into a crowd of people and detonate. In the name of… will cause a woman to destroy an abortion clinic and kill every soul within. In the name of… will continue to take a life off of this planet every 30 seconds. That's right; someone dies as a direct result of In the name of… every 30 seconds.

How many Christians, not just the Klansman Christians, but how many Christians invoke "in the name of Jesus" as they proclaim to control whatever they're making an attempt to control by invoking "in the name of Jesus" while throwing a flaming cross across someone's lawn.

Christian Craft… you know like witchcraft. It's a trip. It doesn't work consistently! Remember what was said earlier: 1 plus 1 equals 2 on Monday, Tuesday, Wednesday, and so on. It always equals 2 because it's a true statement.

The reason why this doesn't work consistently is because it was not meant to be an incantation that was spoken in the European language: "In the name of Jesus." In the name of…means by the "**Authority**", I do this deed. In politics, "**Authority**" (Latin *auctoritas*, used in Roman law as opposed to *potestas* and *imperium*) is often used interchangeably with the term "**Power**". However, their meanings differ in that "**Authority**" is power and the legal right to act, wrapped up in one. While "**Power**" refers to the ability to achieve certain ends and results; again **"Authority"** refers to the legitimacy, justification and right to exercise that **"Power"**.

You must be authorized to speak with the tongues of Angels. You must be authorized to speak things into existence in order to have a **"Quantum Manifestation"**. One must advance to the knowledge of sound, the magical properties that sound presents and the order for which sounds bind this universe together. Einstein states that $E=mc^2$ (Energy = mass vibrating at the speed of light, Squared) and yet the masses are content with his findings on energy, but I tell you on this day, that the sounds you make binds those energy particles together.   There is so much to Quantum Manifestation that will be explored in the next study or sequel: **"Searching for NOD"**.

You see most of the individuals who do things in the name of... have neither the authority or power to achieve such an event, which is why 1 plus 1 does not equal 2 consistently for these individuals **and** when they invoke the term in the name of Jesus, it does not work.

> Then certain of the vagabond Jews, exorcists, took upon them to call over them which had evil spirits the name of the Lord Jesus, saying, We adjure you by Jesus whom Paul preacheth.
>
> And there were seven sons of [one] Sceva, a Jew, [and] chief of the priests, which did so.
>
> And the evil spirit answered and said, Jesus I know, and Paul I know; but who are ye?
>
> And the man in whom the evil spirit was leaped on them, and overcame them, and prevailed against them, so that they fled out of that house naked and wounded.
>
> And this was known to all the Jews and Greeks also dwelling at Ephesus; and fear fell on them all, and the name of the Lord Jesus was magnified. (Acts 19:13-17)

The untruths propagated by the church were meant to strip the Lost Sheep from its power source. If someone states to you, "by this authority, this will save you," or "by this authority, this will heal you," and it does not take place, **then it is a lie**. Not that those things don't happen, but the way they are telling the masses how it happens is the lie. The truth holds a consistent pattern people. The Messiah said Heaven and earth will pass away, but his words will never pass away:

> **Heaven** and **earth** will pass away, but my words will never pass away. (Matthew 24:35)

According to the Bible if the Messiah said it, then it will happen with no exceptions! Again, I said it earlier, you must abide in the Messiah, and the Messiah must abide in you. Then, and only then, will you be able to invoke, according to the Bible that is. You will be able to speak with tongues of angels, or better, the dialect that spoke this universe into existence; a proclamation that states to a mountain be removed, and it will...in the name of. Well, if the spirit of the Messiah is in you, nothing can reject his authority. King of Kings and Lord of Lords, remember? Don't forget.

Now the evil ones have power also. Make no mistake. The empowered evil ones can say mountain be removed and that mountain will be removed. Oh yeah. Make no mistake about it. Not the lower level imps and gimps, but the high level ones, the **real Grand Dragons**, not the demonically oppressed peons running around in sheets burning crosses.

By now I assume that you have sat this book down, picked it up, pondered, and researched what has been written, picked up the book again and pondered again, which is great because there is more. Up until now I've been using the name of Christ, because I know that many of you were not in position to receive the entire unfolding of the Truth about the Messiah, but I must disclose to you more on why, when using "in the name of..." it doesn't work. If you are not paying attention to what you're saying, then you continue to invoke with out power, or shall I say you are calling upon a pagan god.

I previously shared with you about the synagogues of Satan, and how those that call themselves Jews and are not, they are people of

Greek decent. Now, similar to the paganism and Hellenistic propagation of false information, I am left to tell you something that may be disturbing.

Similar to the foregoing components of Sun-worship which had been adopted into the church, in which the Sabbath was changed from Saturday to Sunday Worship, we have proof of the adoption of pagan words and deities, although less convincing of its absolute solar origin. However, we can clearly see that, with the Greeks using Christos (a translation) for the Hebrew Mashiach (Anointed), the word Christos was far more acceptable to the pagans of Greek origin who were worshipping in Creston while shouting "Chrestos"; the worshipping of Chrestos was so intense that a city was named after their deities in Crestonia.

Crestonia (or **Crestonice**) was an ancient region immediately north of Mygdonia. The Echeidorus river, which flowed through Mygdonia into the Thematic Gulf, had its source in Crestonia. It was partly occupied by a remnant of the Pelasgi, who spoke a different language from their neighbors (Thracians and Paionians; later Macedonians and Hellenes). The main towns of Crestonia were **Creston** (*Crestone*) and "Gallicum" (Romanized name). The region, along with Mygdonia, was held by Paionians for a time, later by Thracians. At the time of the invasion of Xerxes I of Persia, Crestonia was ruled by an independent Thracian prince (Herodotus, 8. 116). By the time of the commencement of the Peloponnesian war, Crestonia had been annexed to the kingdom of Macedon. Today, ancient Crestonia is comprehended within the prefectures of Kakis and part of north Thessalonica in Greece.

The Hebrew word Mashiach has been translated in the Old Testament of the King James Version as "Anointed" in most places, but as "Messiah" in two places, namely Dan. 9:25 and 26. This word is a title, although it was used as an appellative (name) later on. Thus, this word was faithfully translated as "Anointed" in the Old Testament and only in Dan 9:25 and 26 was its Hebrew character retained in the transliterated "Messiah". Likewise, we find that the Greeks also admitted their transliterated form Messias in the Greek New Testament in John 1:41 and John 4:25. Why then did they introduce or use the word Christos in the rest of the Greek New Testament? Even if they had preferred Christos to Messias, why did our translators transliterate the word as "Christ"?

Why did they not transliterate the word Messiah, as was done in Daniel 9:25 and 26, seeing that the Greeks had also accepted their Greek transliteration of the word, namely Messias in John 1:41 and John 4:25?

My research into this matter has produced some revealing similarities between Christos and certain pagan names and titles. F.D. Gearly, writing in The Interpreter's Dictionary of the Bible, vol. 1, pp. 571-572, says, "the word Christos ... was easily confused with the common Greek proper name Chrestos, meaning '**good**'." He also quotes a French theological dictionary which says, "It is absolutely beyond doubt that Christus and Chrestus, Christiani and Chrestiani, were used indifferently by the profane and Christian authors of the first two centuries of our era." he continues, "in Greek, 'e' and 'i' were similarly pronounced and often confused, the original spelling of the word should be determined only if we could fix its provenance (origin).

We have already seen that **Chrestos was a common Greek proper name, meaning "good"**. Further, we see in the Realencylcopaedie, commonly called the "Pauly-Wissowa", under "Chrestos", that the inscription Chrestos is to be seen on a **Mithras relief** in the **Vatican**. We also read in J.M. Robertson, Christianity and Mythology, p. 331, **that Osiris, the Sun-deity of Egypt, was reverenced as Chrestos**. We also read of the heretic Gnostics who used the name Chrestos. The confusion and syncretism, is further evidenced by the oldest Christian building known, the Synagogue of the Marionettes on Mt. Hermon, built in the 3rd century, where the Messiah's title or appellation is spelled Chrestos.

Do you hear what I am saying? This is earth shattering! My world was crumbling all around me, as if I was a character in the movie Matrix as I did this research. You think I'm being hard on the Catholics, Protestant, the Greeks, or the Evil Ones? Give me a break.

Justin Martyr (about 150 C.E.) said that Christians were Chrestoi or "good". Tertullian and Lactantius inform us that "the common people usually called Christ Chrestos". Clement of Alexandria, in the same age, said, "All who believe in Christ are called Chrestoi, which is 'good men.'"

The Kingdom is not preached because of chrestoi. The increase need to experience your relationship with God through your god works and restrictive behaviors like ascetism.

The rituals of Sun God Osiris, the Christ (chrestos) who is worshipped on Sunday has carried over into the Protestant church as we know it in America. The church has confused what is holy with what is nice, and pleasing, and what they call good or Chrestos. They blind you with smiles and fake niceness, and propagate how you can be a Good Samaritan. Why? because these pagans have given the world another pagan religion called Christianity, the religion of worshiping the Sun God Osiris as the decoy, and stating to its members that they are worshipping Yahushúa Mashiach but hey, let's just call him Jesus the Christ and the masses won't question it. If they do, well just say that God has many names, they won't know the difference.

Though many truths about Yahushúa Mashiach are located in many of Greek writings, they work feverishly to locate, collect, and destroy the documents and practice of worship. These pagans hate people of color to such a level that they shot the noses off the Sphinx and many other statues in Egypt. I don't even have to tell you what was done to the African American, or the South African. They create shipping embargos, and starve the masses, and when some courageous freedom fighters buck the oppression, they call them terrorists, or the "axis of evil".

Millions are being slaughtered in Africa, and millions are being injected with AIDS and left to die. But we are not nation builders, right? The Church is clearly Under Siege. So many people worship Yahushúa Mashiach who are genuine, loving people working hard everyday to be good, and mind you, a good Christian... as they say. But your leaders (I'm not just talking about the pastor you know), but the Man and/or the Bishop above him, or even the Bishop above the Bishop, this evil lies in high rankings and these are the ones who must be watched—who you must be aware of.

Thus, we can readily see that the word "Christos" was easier to convert the pagans with than the word "Messiah", especially because of the anti-Judaism that prevailed among the pagans. Similar anti-Judaism with the Catholic's, The KKK, The Mormon Church, The Pentecostal Movement, the Assemblies of God, and on and on. There are so many others working against the Hebrew descendants and those that possess the true Spiritual DNA that definitely goes across the color lines. These people snarl at people of color especially the true Hebrews. Don't you dare speak Aramaic like my Lord Yahushúa Mashiach. Don't you dare be a person of color?

94

Even though true Spiritual DNA is broad and without color lines, their hatred for the real descendants of man runs deep. And still today, not many people know why people of color have been despised through out history.

Serapis was another Sun-deity who superseded Osiris in Alexandria. Once again, we must neither falter nor stumble over this confusion among the Gentiles. We must worship the Father in Spirit and in Truth. We do desire to return to the original Scriptures of the New Testament, as far back as we possibly can. As previously mentioned, the Greeks changed Elijah into Helias in the Greek New Testament, and the Helios-worshippers must have been overjoyed because of their Sun-deity being assimilated to the Elijah of the Scriptures. To avoid the confusion between Helias and Helios, we should abide by the Hebrew "Elijah". Likewise, to avoid confusion between Christos and Chrestos, we should abide by the word Anointed - remembering that Osiris the Sun-deity, amongst others, was called Chrestos.

Next we will cover the Old Testament, the canonized scriptures and then some. I hope that this research has touched you in positive way, and I know that many of you have "awakened". Bear with me, for there will be many that will work to suppress this research. Don't be surprised if "they" put forth million dollar campaigns, or if the author will be dragged through the streets, or found in court on some trumped up charges or whatever they can try to impose to keep this away from the public. I have been passionate about my research and it needs to be shared, even if it costs me my life. May my daughters forgive me for such a sacrifice? Let us continue.

THE OLD TESTAMENT
Chapter 5

In the beginning God created the heaven and the earth.

And the earth was without form, and void; and darkness [was] upon the face of the deep. And the Spirit of God moved upon the face of the waters.

And God said, Let there be light: and there was light.

And God saw the light, that [it was] good: and God divided the light from the darkness.

And God called the light Day, and the darkness he called Night. And the evening and the morning were the first day. (Genesis 1:1-5)

In the beginning God created.

I remember reading the King James Version, or Canon #85 back when I was 8 years old. Intrigued by the messages and historical references of man's earlier encounters with God, I found myself comforted by the presence of God and deeply desired to learn more, so I committed to reading the entire Canon #85 from cover to cover. I made it a point to read a chapter a day. Boy, a chapter a day! I can still remember how that felt and I often smile as I reflect on the monumental task that was before me: to read a chapter a day! Compared to now- a- days, it took me sometimes 30 minutes to achieve such a commitment, but I did, at least to the book of Judges. I rejoiced between the Lord and myself after finishing the exhausting book of Genesis and its many chapters, and I remember how my breath was taken away at the site of Exodus chapter 20, when I read with my own eyes the Ten Commandments. To this day I always know where to find the Ten Commandments because of my experience as an 8 year old.

I've enjoyed reading the Bible since I was old enough to understand and able to reason. I mean that! My memory goes way back to things from when I was in my mother's womb. I tell you no lie. My parents can attest to the fact that I have shared this recollection with them.

What a man recalls, and further more, what a man documents has a way of standing the test of time. What a man documents outlives the verbal testimony of one's character and experiences. This is why when it was proposed that I go to visit the Dead Sea Scrolls Exhibit in San Diego in November of 2007, I leapt at the invite.

I could see the actual scrolls with my own eyes; it was like being 8 all over again. However, the experience I had at 41 was not the same, but proved necessary nonetheless. Maybe I should explain: it was a surreal experience, and the majority of the crowd was 99% Jewish (or Grecian Jew if you want to be exact). Where were the Christians? Why were my co-author and I counted as 2 of the 6 Christians interested in the Dead Sea Scrolls that particular day or at least for the 2 o'clock showing? Hmmmmm. It's interesting how written history normally carries more weight than verbal history. You see, anyone can tell you anything, but why is it that individuals will take a verbal statement and qualify it with written statements, thus concluding measurements of validity?

A minister can say anything while at the pulpit but the crowd will find itself comparing or at least seeking written confirmation/validation of what the minister is saying to follow.

That's profound, and human behavior has proven that this measurement of validation and comparing what is said to what is written seems consistent. So, when it was time to examine the writings of the Dead Sea Scrolls, I wanted to make sure I had my thinking cap on.

We were expecting to read confirmation of the truth behind the scriptures and excited about nothing being lost in translation, similar to what we have heard through out the years coming from the pulpit and the media.

But on our way back to Los Angeles my co-author was sharing her views with me. It was astounding how she and I were both in quiet reflection as we drove north on the 5 freeway, when suddenly she burst out...

"As a little girl, I went to traditional church regularly and later, off and on as a teenager at the request of a relative, but I started "hearing" at the age of 18; I was "baptized" at the age of 19. This baptism had no impact on my life and was actually a dunk in the water. I was unaware that baptism was for the forgiveness of sins and that I was to rise to a new life and therefore, I continued to live as before.

"A few months prior to turning 20, things really changed for me: I began to pray all day every day, for months and months. I was always talking to God in my head and when I would get off of the bus from work or school I would be walking down the street talking to my God without a care of who thought I was loony. I began reading my Bible on my own without much success. At the age of 21, I completely dove into my Bible like a radical Jesus freak, made 180 degree changes, got baptized and the rest is history. In the last 13 years I have had the privilege of spending hours upon hours upon hours in what I proclaimed to be God's word and witnessing hundreds of heart conversions and life changes.

"I am totally against church traditions, but I developed my own traditions. 2007 has been a year of

breaking those traditions and getting my sold out, unshakable mind and heart unglued from what 'I believe' to be truth. Although I have plenty of examples I'll only mention the Dead Sea Scrolls.

"I've always thought the Dead Sea Scrolls (DSS) were a confirmation of what is in the Scriptures. Yea! The Bible is really true and has been preserved the way God intended. These ancient findings support and match what we've believed to be true all along. But this is not what I found. What impressed me the most was that there were no contradictions found in **Isaiah**: a book referred to several times in the New Testament and in which there are prophecies that are fulfilled in the New Testament. In Job, the Aramaic translation deviates from the Hebrew translation, which brings questions of what was actually intended to be written. Also there are writings that I'm unfamiliar with and called un-received text."

I was floored by how the exhibit had affected us both in practically the same manner. But far from the case, the Dead Sea Scrolls (or DSS) were primarily about the men who found the scrolls; the timeline that gave validation to those documents; the location, the city of Qumran; how the scribes lived; and who could have possibly visited this site, namely Jesus, Peter, and Paul.

It was exciting to see such an exhibit although it didn't come without its controversy. Of course, similar to the New Testament "ghost

  writers", the DSS had many books from scribes tucked away in vases found in caves. There were scriptures from Leviticus, Deuteronomy, Job, Isaiah, The Book of War, The Book of Enoch and of course there were more scriptures, writings, and commentaries. Qumran was a place for scribes to manually replicate the work of what was and still is perceived as the Holy Scriptures. This is a picture of the remnants of the Book of Leviticus. According to the exhibit, it is called the Paleo-Hebrew version of

Leviticus, and along with the scriptures from Deuteronomy, one possessed the validation that would be sought... when searching for the truth, that is.

In order to examine the History of the Old Testament and use it as a qualifier for the scriptures in the New Testament, you would have to start at the beginning at what many call the Books of Moses. As you have heard throughout the ages, the Books of Moses are the first 5 books published in the received text from the Catholic Church: Genesis, Exodus, Leviticus, Numbers, and Deuteronomy.

Did Moses write the first five books? Why was this mistruth propagated? Well, if you write it down and have an important individual of authority proclaim the documents to be what ever he or she stated they are then, who can argue it? If a judge says you are guilty, then verdict is rendered. Right or wrong, just or not, it does not matter: the verdict is in.

The same concept applies here. If you have a priest of the Levitical Order make a proclamation, then "so shall it be." There are many measurements of evidence stating that Moses, though a phenomenal leader and prophet, did not write his own autobiography. According to research, the Deuteronomist and some of the Levites wrote the first five books. Do you believe that Moses and Machiavelli had something in common? Did they predict their own deaths, let alone write books documenting their deaths and the responses coming from the environment after death?

> *And the LORD said unto him, This [is] the land which I sware unto Abraham, unto Isaac, and unto Jacob, saying, I will give it unto thy seed: I have caused thee to see [it] with thine eyes, but thou shalt not go over thither.*
>
> *So Moses the servant of the LORD died there in the land of Moab, according to the word of the LORD. (Deuteronomy 34:4-5)*

I don't think so.

The Messiah? Yeah, I can see that. Moses? Naw. So why would this be propagated? Why was it important to let the masses believe such a lie as "Moses wrote the first five books"?

Hey, the awesomeness of God is overwhelming within itself. We need not plagiarize or lie to validate. Or do we?

If you want control, if you want to write yourself into history, if you want to be a **gatekeeper**, then, Oh yeah, you will. You will plagiarize and promote yourself as a go between in between God and his creation, man.

It is also rumored and believed by many that these books were written by Moses and the established laws come from such books.

People like **Dr. Julius Wellhausen** (May 17, 1844 - January 7, 1918), was a German biblical scholar and Orientalist in the early 1900's. He tackled this same question and worked on the history of the people of Israel.

He was famous for his critical investigations into Old Testament history and the composition of the *Hexateuch*, the uncompromising scientific attitude he adopted in testing its problems, creating an antagonistic relationship with the older school of biblical interpreters. He is perhaps most well-known for his *Prolegomena zur Geschichte Israel's* of 1883 (first published 1878 as *Geschichte Israel's*), in which he advanced a definitive formulation of the Documentary hypothesis, arguing that **the Torah or Pentateuch had its origins in a redaction of four originally independent texts dating from several centuries after the time of Moses, their traditional author.** Wellhausen's hypothesis remained the dominant paradigm for Pentateuchal studies until the last quarter of the 20th century, when it began to be challenged by scholars who saw more and more hands at work in the Torah, ascribing them to periods **even later** than Wellhausen had proposed.

Julius Wellhausen and his colleague Martin Noth have reported traces of the earlier Jahwist communities and Elohist communities as sources in to the first books of Canon #85. Both Noth and Wellhausen argued that the books of the Pentateuch should be considered as a unit with the book of Joshua creating a 'Hexateuch' not Pentateuch. It is mostly understood in *Prolegomena zur Geschichte Israels*.

Well the subject of the *Prolegomena* is the origins of the Pentateuch. It reviews all the major advances of the preceding century by Johann Gottfried Eichhorn, Wilhelm de Wette, Karl Heinrich Graf and others, and puts forward the author's view, which is that the priestly source was the last of the four sources, written during the Babylonian exile c.550 BC. The implication to be drawn from this was that the Mosaic Law contained in Leviticus, which is largely by the priestly author, as well as the substantial amounts of material from the priestly source to be found in Genesis, Exodus and the Book of Numbers, did not exist in the age of Joshua, Samuel, David and Solomon.

The book consists of an author's introduction and three major sections. Its argument is that the ancient Israelites did not practice a religion recognizable as Judaism: the earliest religion of the Israelites, as depicted in the Yahwist and Elohist sources, was polytheistic and family-based; the middle layer, the Deuteronomist, shows a clear impulse to the centralization of worship under the control of a dominant priesthood with royal support; and only in the final, post-Exilic layer, the priestly source, when the royal authority had vanished and the priesthood had assumed sole authority over the community, is there evidence of the religion which the world knows as Judaism today.

Each of the sources - Yahwist/Elohist, Deuteronomist and Priestly - reflects a different stage in evolution of religious practice in ancient Israel. Thus, to take one of the five, the Yahwist/Elohist "sanctions a multiplicity of altars", allowing sacrifice at any place; the Deuteronomist records the moment in history (i.e., the reform of Josiah, c.620 BC), when a single place of worship was demanded by both priesthood and king; and the **Priestly law-code** does not demand, but **presupposes centralized worship.** In the same way the other elements of ancient Israelite religion - sacrifice, sacred feasts, the position of the priests and Levites, and the "endowment of the clergy" (tithes due to the priests and Levites) - have a radically different form in the Yahwist/Elohist to those in the Priestly source, with Deuteronomy occupying an intermediate position. The Priestly source consistently attempts to disguise what are in fact innovations with a veneer of antiquity, inventing, for example, a fictional Tabernacle not mentioned anywhere in the oldest sources, to justify its insistence on centralized worship in Jerusalem. "What is brought forward in Deuteronomy as an innovation is assumed in the Priestly Code to be an ancient custom dating as far back as to Noah."

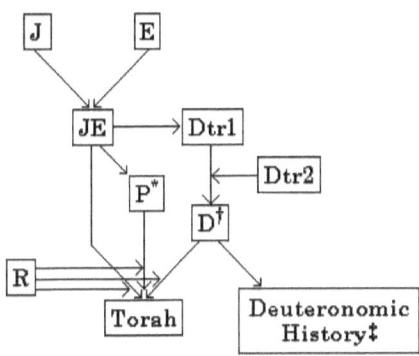

* Includes most of Leviticus
† Includes most of Deuteronomy
‡ Joshua, Judges, 1 & 2 Samuel, 1 & 2 Kings

The **documentary hypothesis (DH)** proposes that the first five books of the Old Testament (Genesis, Exodus, Leviticus, Numbers and Deuteronomy, known collectively as the Torah or Pentateuch), represent a combination of documents from four originally independent sources:

- The J, or Jahwist, source; (The name Yahweh begins with a J in Wellhausen's native German).
- The E, or Elohist, source;
- Dhe D, or Deuteronomist, source;

- The P, or <u>Priestly</u>, source.

The editor who combined the sources into the final Pentateuch is known as R, for <u>Redactor</u>.

The four sources

- **J** — the *Jahwist*. The oldest source, concerned with narratives, making up half of Genesis and the first half of Exodus, plus fragments of Numbers. J describes a human-like God, called Yahweh (or rather YHWH) throughout, and has a special interest in the territory of the Kingdom of Judah and individuals connected with its history. J has an extremely eloquent style. Originally composed c 950 BC.

- **E** — the *Elohist*. E parallels J, often duplicating the narratives. Makes up a third of Genesis and the first half of Exodus, plus fragments of Numbers. E describes a human-like God initially called *Elohim*, and *Yahweh* subsequent to the incident of the burning bush, at which Elohim reveals himself as Yahweh. E focuses on the Kingdom of Israel and on the Shiloh priesthood, has a moderately eloquent style. Originally composed c 850 BC.

- **D** — the *Deuteronomist*. D takes the form of a series of sermons about the Law, and consists of most of Deuteronomy. Its distinctive term for God is *YHWH Elohainu*, translated in English as "The Lord our God." Originally composed c 650-621 BCE.

- **P** — the *Priestly* source. Preoccupied with the centrality of the priesthood, and with lists (especially genealogies), dates, numbers and laws. P describes a distant and unmerciful God, referred to as *Elohim*. P partly duplicates J and E, but alters details

104

to stress the importance of the priesthood. P consists of about a fifth of Genesis, substantial portions of Exodus and Numbers, and almost all of Leviticus. P has a low level of literary style. Composed c 550-400 BC.

Prior to the 17th century both Jews and Christians accepted the traditional view that Moses had written down the Torah under the direct inspiration—even dictation—of God. A few rabbis and philosophers asked how Moses could have described his own death, or given a list of the kings of Edom before those kings ever lived, **but none doubted the truth of the tradition, for the purpose of scholarship 'was to underline the antiquity and authority of the teaching in the Pentateuch, not to demonstrate who wrote the books.**

Now the Jahwist's story begins much earlier than the Elohist's; in fact, it begins at the beginning. Consequently, it introduces stories concerning the general human condition, both large tales such as Adam and Eve, Cain and Abel, as well as brief stories, like that of the Curse of Ham, and the tower of Babel. It also includes general creation stories, such as that of creation itself, the flood, and the badly truncated, and thus difficult to interpret, story of the Nephilim.

In the texts of Ugarit, there were 70 sons of God, each one being the special deity of a particular people from whom they were descended. Some memory of this is found in Biblical texts which speak of Baal Melkart of Tyre or Chemosh of Moab.

The story of the Nephilim is chronicled more fully in the Book of Enoch (part of Ethiopian biblical canon). Enoch, as well as Jubilees, connects the origin of the Nephilim with the fallen angels, and in particular with the Grigori (*watchers*). Samyaza, an angel of high rank, is described as leading a rebel sect of angels in a descent to earth to instruct humans in righteousness. The tutelage went on for a few centuries, but soon the angels pined for the human females and began to instruct the women in magic and conjuring. The angels consummated their lust, and as a result produced hybrid offspring: the Nephilim.

According to these texts, the fallen angels who begat the Nephilim were cast into Tartarus/Gehenna, a place of 'total darkness'. However, Jubilees also states that God granted ten percent of the disembodied spirits of the Nephilim to remain after the flood, as demons, to try to lead the human race astray (through idolatry, the occult, etc.) until the final Judgement.

In addition to *Enoch*, the *Book of Jubilees* (7:21-25) also states that ridding the Earth of these Nephilim was one of God's purposes for flooding the Earth in Noah's time. The Biblical reference to Noah being "perfect in his generations" may have referred to his having a clean, Nephilim-free bloodline, although it may be inferred that there was more diversity among his three daughters-in law. So if you remember what was said in chapter 1:

> *More than one type of human is walking this earth: (a) There are people ordained from the beginning of time containing Spiritual DNA, fully capable of receiving the word of God, who carry themselves accordingly, (b) those individuals who are rotten to the core, who look like us, talk like us, are not human, but carry the likeness of human flesh, and (c) cross breeds who are the product of man, who find themselves accepting their fate similar to an embryo accepting its gender. A cross breed is the type of individual that you would most likely find walking this earth. It gets cloudy for people when it comes to being able to discern the company they keep. While observing an inconsistency in the character of surrounding individuals, most observers give the benefit of the doubt and reach out to influence those surrounding them to conduct themselves in the manner that the Messiah, Paul and others have stated. Again, like an embryo accepting its gender, the cross breed would lean toward one side of the spectrum or the other, regardless of the campaigns given by accompanying individuals who continue to reprove their companions with possible improvements, but let's continue with Dr. Wellhausen's discovery...*

You see there are also allusions to these descendants in the deuterocanonical books of *Judith*, *Sirach*, *Baruch*, *3 Maccabees*, and *Wisdom of Solomon*...origins of contaminated blood and Spiritual DNA.

But you must continue to have the courage to examine clues that lead you toward the truth. He that has an ear is the difference between the "red pill" and the "blue pill". Well, the information from the Dead Sea Scrolls was engaging and lead us toward the true writers of the beginning of the Bible courtesy of Julius Wellhausen, which still stands today without credible resistance. But when you explore what the Catholic Church worked hard to suppress about the Nephilim and other books and writings you cannot continue to stay in the world of belief with out committing to becoming a part of the world of knowing. This can be expedited by exploring the work of Gerald Massey.

It has been stated that Massey, although he might have been considered a Christian Socialist, was in actuality a practicing Druid, presumably a neo-druid. Not only that, Massey was elected Chosen Chief of the Most Ancient Order of Druids from 1880 through 1906. This assessment contrasts strongly with the description of him quoted just below by a friend and colleague, who praised him *for having thrown off the constraints of religion in favor of science and philosophy for the advancement of knowledge.*

But was that assessment accurate? It's amazing what happens when you become a key to the pathway toward the truth. The system will create a label for in order to create doubt or to discredit whatever you might find.

Gerald Massey was a spiritualist and studied many religions in search of the truth. He wrote many documents and a host of books containing   beacons of truth like, **THE HISTORIC JESUS, AND THE MYTHICAL CHRIST, THE BOOK OF THE BEGININGS, ANCIENT EGYPT: The Light of the World.** Although previously accused of being a white person caught up in afrocentrism, he documented his findings as **Truth.** It's not about how black your skin is. It's about Spiritual DNA. Remember spiritual DNA exists regardless of color of skin or origin of birth. If a donkey walked up and spoke English to you and warned you of the truth of something would you heed to the message or would the donkey need to look like a two-year-old Anglo-Saxon baby with wings before you would believe that the message was from God?

You see, those Greco's (those with a Hellenizing spirit) are everywhere. They have infiltrated each and every religious order walking the earth. They started Christianity, infiltrated The Ancient Order of Druids, the Neo-Druids, the Israeli government, the U.S. Government, the Egyptian Mystery System, well not quite but they are working feverishly to unlock the codes. I challenge you to pick a religion, research it and see if it has not been Hellenized by the Greeks.

Remember Hitler? What was he trying to exterminate? Why did he work so passionately and so hard to destroy the so called Grecian Jews and people of any color, especially Africans? (Remember Hitler refusing to shake the hands of the African American men who won Olympics gold medals in Germany?) The Messiah said that a **house divided shall fall**. Could Hitler have set out to exterminate a rival order in the Grecian Jews? As heinous as his crimes against humanity were, you still have to ask, **"What motivated him to commit such atrocity? What did he know?"**

You had two evil forces that did not work harmoniously, so one chose to destroy the other in order to create more harmony in its attempt to create a new and complete world order.

Hitler was overly concerned about the mixing of bloodlines. He even chose to mate with a relative to keep his bloodline pure. Could he have been part of the purely evil blood line mentioned earlier in the book? Hey- if you can't eliminate or differentiate between pure evil and greatly compromised evil then you are left with exterminating them all.

"Kill them all", said Hitler. Kill them all.

The Holocaust (from the Greek Ὁλόκαυστον (holókauston): holos, "completely" and kaustos, "burnt"), also known as **Ha-Shoah** (Hebrew:

האושה), **Churben** (Yiddish: חורבן), is the term generally used to
describe the killing of approximately six million European Jews during
World War II, as part of a program of deliberate extermination
planned and executed by the National Socialist regime in Germany
led by Adolf Hitler.

Holos means **completely**, **Kaustos** means **burnt**. Hmmmmm.....
Holocaust comes from the Greek? Well you have got to be kidding
me! Do people really think that those who call themselves Jews and
are not but of Greek descent would continue to chant Greek words?
Remember the Holocaust? Why not remember Ha Shoah? People
come on! I know the obvious does not elude you.

Hitler had a famous symbol: the **swastika** (from Sanskrit *svástika*),
which is an equilateral cross with its arms bent at right angles, in
either right-facing or left-facing forms. The swastika can also be
drawn as a traditional swastika, but with a second 90° bend in each
arm. The term is derived from Sanskrit *svasti*, meaning well-being.

Archaeological evidence of swastika-shaped ornaments dates from
the Neolithic period. An ancient symbol, it occurs in numerous
indigenous Asian, European, African and Native American cultures;
sometimes as a geometric motif and sometimes as a religious
symbol. It has long been widely used in major world religions such as
Hinduism, Buddhism,
and Jainism.

Neolithic Period? I've
heard of blue rags and
red rags among Los
Angeles gang
bangers, but you too
Hitler? So the colors
that Hitler drew from
were from the
Neolithic Period,
dating back to a
Neolithic culture which appeared in the Levant (Jericho, modern-
day West Bank) about 8500 BC. It developed directly from the
Epipaleolithic Natufian culture in the region, whose people
pioneered wild cereal use, which evolved into true farming. The
Natufians can thus be called "proto-Neolithic" (11,000-8500 BC). As
the Natufians had become dependent on wild cereals in their diet, a

sedentary way of life began and the climatic changes associated with the Younger Dryas forced people to develop farming. By 8500-8000 BC farming communities arose in the **Levant** and spread to **Anatolia, North Africa and North Mesopotamia**.

Do you think two evil factions were not fighting one another? Here you have Hitler sporting colors that come from the Epipaleolithic Natufian culture located in the Levant or modern day West Bank, which we call the Fertile Crescent today.

The war in the Middle East is not a war between Ishmael and Isaac as proclaimed by ministers from the pulpit; it is a war between powers and principalities that fight amongst themselves in a very clandestine manner. It is an underworld of violence that draws members from mankind into it, resulting in untold numbers of uncountable human casualties of war.

The Swastika is found in Hinduism, Buddhism, and Jainism because the origin of the Swastika lies within the order for which it is being worshipped. The Third Reich was and remains closer to the reality of the ones who control these cults. Again, I'm talking Spiritual DNA, not human leadership.

So when you examine Hitler's quest to eradicate a rival order through cremation, or what some would say to **completely burn** the individuals with evil Spiritual DNA, you would still have to examine whether or not the burning of such individuals would be the only method of approaching this one world order. Among the evil cults

 you have different viewpoints regarding how to perfect complete control, which would once again lend itself to search for such religious relics that would empower them. To do so they would do what they have always done when they did not know something--take a trip to Egypt. The church would find itself once again on the cusp of what they would coin a new science, at least to Europe: *the science of alchemy*.

Hitler was not the only one who practiced alchemy, but many of the church's popes and bishops also practiced alchemy. In the history of science, **alchemy** refers to both an early form of the investigation of nature and an early

philosophical and spiritual discipline, both combining elements of chemistry, metallurgy, physics, medicine, astrology, semiotics, mysticism, spiritualism, and art all as parts of one greater force. Alchemy has been practiced in Mesopotamia, Ancient Egypt, Persia, India, Japan, Korea and China, in Classical Greece and Rome, in the Muslim civilization, and then in Europe up to the 19th century—in a complex network of schools and philosophical systems spanning at least 2500 years.

Alchemy as we know it comes from the Legendary Philosopher's Stone that many nations have sought after, and very few have claimed to uncover.

The **philosopher's stone** (Latin: *lapis philosophorum*; Greek: *chrysopoeia*) is a legendary substance, supposedly capable of turning inexpensive metals into gold; it was also sometimes believed to be a means of making people younger, if not making them immortal. For a long time it was the "holy grail" of Western alchemy.

In the view of spiritual alchemy, making the philosopher's stone would bring enlightenment upon the maker and conclude the great work.

Alchemists once thought a key component of the stone was a mythical element named **carmot**. The element is no longer believed to exist according to modern scientific knowledge. *This legendary stone was thought to help amplify transmutations while performing alchemy. It was also thought to have had a dark red tone.*

Alchemy itself is mostly an original concept and science practiced in the ancient Middle East, Egypt, Greece, and India. However, the concept of ensuring youthful health originated in China, while the concept of the transmutation of one metal into a more precious one (silver or gold) originated from the theories of the 8th century Arab alchemist, Jabir ibn Hayyan (Latinized as 'Geber'). He analyzed each Aristotelian element in terms of the four basic qualities of *hotness*, *coldness*, *dryness*, and *moistness*. Fire was both hot and dry, earth cold and dry, water cold and moist, and air hot and moist. He further theorized that every metal was a combination of these four principles, two of them interior and two exterior.

From this premise, it was reasoned that the transmutation of one metal into another could be effected by the rearrangement of its basic qualities. This change would presumably be mediated by a substance, which came to be called *al-iksir* in Arabic (from which the Western term "elixir" is derived). It is often considered to exist as a dry red powder made from a legendary stone — the "philosopher's stone". Keep in mind an elixir is a) an alchemic preparation formerly believed to be capable of prolonging life; b) an alchemic preparation formerly believed to be capable of transmuting base metals into gold;

c) the quintessence or absolute embodiment of anything; and d) a cure-all; a sovereign remedy. The word *alchemy* itself was derived from the **Arabic** word الكيمياء *al-kimia*, which is an important note since the concept of the transmutation of metal originated from the theories 8th century **Arab** alchemist, Jabir ibn Hayyan as mentioned above. We will not omit origins and we will continue to explore origin. You may have noticed a pattern while reading. Some thing, some name, some place, some something originated as one name, but amazingly the original name has been Latinized, Westernized, Canonized, Grecianized or Hellenized in someway. Is there power in origin? Obviously! And the importance of the origin of words will be discussed momentarily.

According to history, the 13th-century scientist and philosopher Saint Albertus Magnus is said to have discovered the philosopher's stone and passed it to his pupil Thomas Aquinas, shortly before his death circa 1280. Magnus does not confirm he discovered the stone in his writings, but he did record that he witnessed the creation of gold by "transmutation".

The 16th-century Swiss alchemist Philippus Paracelsus believed in the existence of alkahest which he thought to be an undiscovered element from which all other elements (earth, fire, water, and air) were simply derivative forms. Paracelsus believed that this element alkahest was, in fact, the philosopher's stone. A potential problem involving alkahest is that, if it dissolves everything, then it cannot be placed into a container, because it would dissolve the container. However, philosopher Philalethe specifies that Alkahest (that he also calls "double mercury" sometime) dissolves only composed material.

Jabir's theory was based on the concept that metals like gold and silver could be hidden in alloys and ores, from which they could be recovered by the appropriate chemical treatment. Jabir himself is believed to be the inventor of aqua regia, a mixture of muriatic (hydrochloric) and nitric acids, one of the few substances that can dissolve gold (and which is still often used for gold recovery and purification).

Gold was particularly valued as a metal that would not rust, tarnish, corrode or otherwise grow corrupt. Since the philosopher's stone would turn a corruptible base metal to incorruptible gold, naturally it would similarly transform human beings from mortal (corruptible) to immortal (incorruptible). One of many theories was that gold was a superior form of metal, and that the philosopher's stone was even

purer and superior to gold, and if combined with lesser metals would turn them into superior gold as well.

A mystical text published in the 17th century called the Mutus Liber appears to be a symbolic instruction manual for concocting a philosopher's stone. Called the "wordless book", it was a collection of 15 illustrations.

The Latin American spiritual teacher Samael Aun Weor stated that the philosopher's stone is synonymous with the symbol of the stone found in many other spiritual and religious traditions, such as the stone Jacob rests his head upon, the cubic stone of Freemasonry, and the rock upon which the Messiah lays the foundation of the temple.

> Wherefore also it is contained in the scripture, Behold, I lay in Sion a chief corner stone, elect, precious: and he that believeth on him shall not be confounded.
>
> Unto you therefore which believe [he is] precious: but unto them which be disobedient, the stone which the builders disallowed, the same is made the head of the corner,

And a stone of stumbling, and a rock of offence, [even to them] which stumble at the word, being disobedient: whereunto also they were appointed. (1 Peter 2: 6-8)

Samael states that this "stone of stumbling" and "rock of offence" is the creative-sexual energy, which in Kabbalah is Yesod ("foundation") that must be transmuted through sexual alchemy. It is said to be rejected by the "builders," meaning those who seek spiritual edification, because they reject the transmutation of sexual energy, and instead use it to achieve sensual pleasure.

Now one of the most famous alchemists not associated with the Church was **Nicolas Flamel** (traditionally c. 1330 – 1417), a successful scrivener and manuscript-seller who developed a reputation as an alchemist due to his work on the Philosopher's Stone.

Flamel was the attributed author of an alchemical book, published in Paris in 1612 as *Livre des figures hiéroglypiques* and in London in 1624 as *Exposition of the Hieroglyphicall Figures*. It is an exposition of figures purportedly commissioned by Flamel for a tympanum at the Cimetière des Innocents in Paris, long disappeared by the time the work was published. In its publisher's introduction Flamel's search for the Philosopher's Stone was described:

Flamel had made it his life's work to understand the text of a mysterious twenty-one-page book he had purchased; the introduction recounts that around 1378, he traveled to Spain for assistance with translation. On the way back, he reported that he met a sage, who identified Flamel's book as being a copy of the

114

original *Book of Abraham* also known as the Codex (at right). With this knowledge, over the next few years Flamel and his wife allegedly decoded enough of the book to successfully replicate its recipe for the Philosopher's Stone, producing first silver in 1382, and then gold.

According to the introduction to his work and the additional details that have accrued since its publication, Flamel would thus have been the most accomplished of the European alchemists, who would have learned his art from a Jewish *converso* on the road to Santiago de Compostela. "Others thought Flamel was the creation of seventeenth-century editors and publishers desperate to produce modern printed editions of supposedly ancient alchemical treatises then circulating in manuscript for an avid reading public," Deborah Harkness put it succinctly. The modern assertion that many references to him or his writings appear in alchemical texts of the 1500s, however, has not been linked to any particular source. **The essence of his reputation is that he succeeded at the two magical goals of alchemy -- that he made the Philosopher's Stone which turns lead into gold, and that he and his wife Perenelle achieved immortality.**

Isn't it amazing how certain people have similar accomplishments and all of them belong to the science of alchemy? Men like Benjamin Franklin, Thomas Jefferson, Sr. Isaac Newton, DaVinci, Nostradamus, Hitler, Albert Einstein and Albertus Magnus. All are accredited with an extensive list of inventions and discoveries that their peers thought were ahead of their time.

I would like to introduce you to Avicenna, a man you may have never heard of, but who I know was also a man ahead of his time. Be amazed at his accomplishments. According to history, in the 11th century, there was a debate among Muslim chemists on whether the transmutation of substances was possible. A leading opponent was Avicenna, who discredited the theory of the transmutation of substances, and we will not ignore him because he discredited a theory. After all, you and I are researching.

Abū Alī al-□usayn ibn Abd Allāh ibn Sīnā
(Persian: ابو علی الحسین بن عبدالله ابن سینا; c. 980 in Bukhara, Khorasan – 1037 in Hamedan), also known as **Ibn Seena** and commonly known in English by his Latinized name

115

Avicenna (Greek Αβιτζιανός), was a Persian Muslim **polymath** and the foremost **physician** and **Islamic philosopher** of his time. He was also an **astronomer, chemist, Hafiz, logician, mathematician, poet, psychologist, physicist, scientist, Sheikh, soldier, statesman** and **theologian**.

Ibn Sīnā wrote almost 450 treatises on a wide range of subjects, of which around **240 have survived**. In particular, 150 of his surviving treatises concentrate on philosophy and 40 of them concentrate on medicine. His most famous works are *The Book of Healing*, a vast philosophical and scientific encyclopedia, and *The Canon of Medicine*, which was a standard medical text at many Islamic and European universities up until the early 19th century. The *Canon of Medicine* was used as a text-book in the universities of Montpellier and Louvain as late as 1650. *Ibn Sīnā developed a medical system that combined his own personal experience with that of Islamic medicine, the medical system of the Greek physician Galen, Aristotelian metaphysics (Avicenna was one of the main interpreters of Aristotle), and ancient Persian, Mesopotamian and Indian medicine.* He was also the founder of **Avicennian logic** and the philosophical school of **Avicennism**, which were influential among both Muslim and Scholastic thinkers.

Why haven't we heard of Ibn Sīnā, also known as Avicenna? Get ready for this! He was also regarded as a **father** of early modern medicine, particularly for **his introduction** of systematic experimentation and quantification into the study of physiology, **his discovery** of the contagious nature of infectious diseases, **the introduction** of quarantine to limit the spread of contagious diseases, **the introduction** of experimental medicine, evidence-based medicine, clinical trials, randomized controlled trials, efficacy tests, clinical pharmacology, neuropsychiatry, risk factor analysis, and **the idea** of a syndrome, and **the importance** of dietetics and **the influence** of climate and environment on health? **He is also considered the father of the fundamental concept of momentum in physics, and regarded as a pioneer of aromatherapy.** *Avicenna proves the importance of origin.*

With the Dead Sea Scrolls; the Elohist's and Yahwist's writings being the foundation for the Pentateuch; many documents of the party religion Christianity initiated by the Greeks (or if you would like to take a step further, the Greco's); we now have overwhelming proof that these Greco's have been working hard to misdirect the Lost Sheep.

Then the Iraq War of 2003; Hitler's quest to exterminate the Jews and being a part of a religious order from the Neolithic period that started 11000 BC; the Nephilim or fallen angels dating back way before the chronological King James Version, or Canon #85; the Pentateuch and other writings all provide incontrovertible, undeniable evidence of what is being said in this discussion between me and you. I have discovered that the Old Testament is a truncated work of scriptures that was and still is used to mislead the masses. You will find many truths within them, and you will read many plagiarized commentaries, as you will discover when you read more on the works of Gerald Massey and Julius Wellenhausen. I will write a book about the more extensive work on the Old Testament later, but for the sake of the Lost Sheep I wanted to touch on how the Old Testament was used as a qualifier for the New Testament with Christian trappings.

Now that you know Jesus' real name was Yahushúa, and that he spoke Aramaic, I would like to ask you to go ask your ministers, friends, family, or whoever you think may know the answer to this question: What were the Hebrew names for the 12 disciples? Now let me guess at a few responses you may receive. All of them may tell you it is not important. Maybe they will tell you the Greek names for these individuals. But that's not the question, is it? What are the Hebrew or Jewish names for the disciples? They have to know the answer, right? Only Yahushúa has a Hebrew name, now why is that? Why is it that all of a sudden the 12 disciples disappear from the face of the earth, unless you focus on the Greek accountings, or Greek Testaments now known as the New Testament, which was written by Greeks? No Hebrew writings prior to the Greek that could give you this information. Just the European names: Thomas, Mark, Luke, John, Peter. Something, something, something, something just ain't right.

This is an examination of history. We cannot treat belief like history; we must treat history like history, thus rendering the treatment of historical fact more valuable than traditional belief. We must uncover available answers as we discover manifesting secrets and put an end to the myth that sacred information must remain a mystery. The cries to abandon and the screech of alerts to prevent individuals from traversing beyond a traditional belief system are suppressing the mimetics of society.

117

Are you starting to get the picture? I guess facts and the truth are not important, believing is important, not the truth. I don't think so. The truth is always important. What you and I are doing is searching for discoverable answers, which are the very things that ministers tell us do not exist. Or don't worry about that, just believe. If the truth about these mysteries exists and it's within our reach, then we should grab it and free ourselves from the abyss of ignorance where the **only** choice we have is to "believe".

REVEALED
Chapter 6

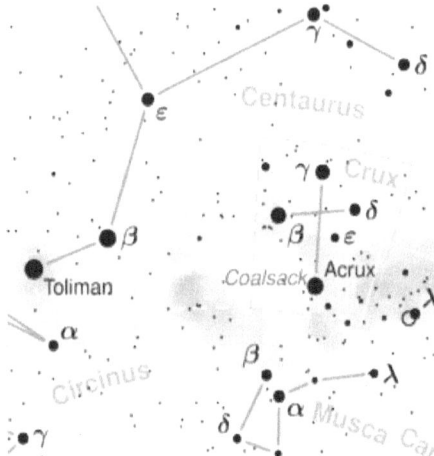

I have shared many things with you and I am proud of you. You have made it this far without turning from my discoveries. With great pleasure I can say that you have graduated to a new level of understanding. Now let us proceed with your graduate studies.

When I was a child, my parents held church at our home where we sang hymns and worshipped God. It was fun. One of my best memories is of the times when we started to sing hymns. My cousin Jamie and I would look at each other sometimes with psychic predictability about how we knew church was going to start. I remember one of the mothers from the church, Sister Davis, would start one of two songs and everyone else would follow suit with either This **Little Light of Mine (I'm going to let it shine....) or At the Cross, at the cross where I first saw the light, and the burdens of my heart rolled away, rolled away. For it was there by faith I received my sight, and now I am happy all the day!**

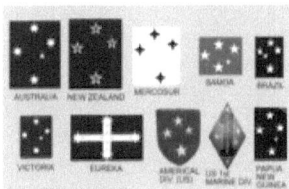

The best way to sum up this exploration we're sharing is to end with the proclaimed beginning of Christianity: at the Cross. We have seen throughout the centuries that the number one symbol for Christianity is the Cross. I have shared that the religion we call Christianity is designed to control the masses while having its members worship a make believe deity called Jesus or Mithra, who is an offshoot of Horus, the son of Osiris, the Egyptian Sun

119

Deity. This all came from the Greek culture, conjured up by Grecian pagans and Grecian Jews with the majority (if not all) of the New Testament being translated from the Greek. Now let's examine the Cross, better known as the Crux.

Crux (pronounced /□krʌks/, Latin: cross), commonly known as the **Southern Cross** (*Crux Australis*, in contrast to the Northern Cross), is the smallest of the 88 modern constellations, but nevertheless one of the most distinctive. It is surrounded on three sides by the constellation Centaurus while to the south lies the *Fly* (Musca). Ancient Greeks originally thought Crux was part of Centaurus, but it was defined as a separate asterism in the 16th century after Amerigo Vespucci's expedition to South America in 1501.

Vespucci mapped the two stars, Alpha Centauri and Beta Centauri as well as the stars of the Crux. Although these stars were known to the ancient Greeks, gradual precession of the equinoxes had lowered them below the European skyline so that they were forgotten there. For example at the latitude of Athens in 1000 B.C., the Crux was clearly visible, although it was low in the sky. However, by 400 A.D., most of the constellation never rose above the horizon for Athenians.

The significance of this Crux is reflected in many flags of many nations. Remember Hitler donning his colors and the Swastika? Well, many of the nations don their colors in similar ways. These nations having being Hellenized, don their colors for the house of Wicca that they belong to. Australia, New Zealand, and Brazil are controlled by the same secret societies. You see the stars in the flags represent something. Make no mistake about it, even "Old Glory" possesses lineage.

Back to the Crux; The earth lines up with the four stars of the winter solstice, the bright star Sirus and the trailing stars known as the three kings, which gives you the tale of the Three Wiseman that followed the bright star which led them to the Messiah. **It was at the cross, at the cross, where I first saw the light,** remember that? Canon #85 tells us that the Messiah bore all of our burdens on the cross and eliminated the consequences of sin. According to the origins of these Sun worshipers, the winter solstice presents itself and the process starts when the earth lines up on December 22 of each year and by the end of December 24th, Sirus aligns with the three kings in Orion's Belt.

From the winter solstice till the summer solstice, the sun appears to travel further from the earth until it fades and the Sun disappears **(you can see this depending where on earth you are located)** into the south for three days only to be resurrected to live once again in the heavens. The resurrection of the sun is mostly celebrated on the end of this period, which was and is still celebrated among its Sun worshipers including the Christian sect of sun worshipers, on Easter. This is why it is said that the Son of God died on the Cross and was resurrected on the third day. You see, Christianity is a parody religion that stole its concepts from other religions and some truths, including information on Yahushúa Mashiach and because he was a person of color, it was not acceptable to portray him as he truly was. Let's look at how the Greeks portrayed Yahushúa in whom they disguised their pagan influence over the masses while distorting the truth and selling lies for offerings; let's look at what they said Jesus looked like. As you can see Jesus has the Crux symbol behind his head as a hidden message to their own kind, like a secret handshake of sort. In many earlier drawings of Christ and widely circulated in the Middle Ages, Jesus has the Zodiac Circle and the Crux. In some drawings it is subtle, while on others the Zodiac Circle is obvious.

121

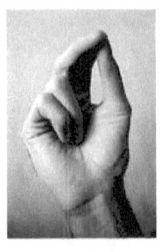  In the Byzantine era the hand symbol of the Crux was used by many. The Greco's coined it, and as many hidden/secret handshakes find themselves exposed, it eventually became widely used by many Christians. The open palm with the index and the middle finger clasped together to symbolize the trinity was later displayed and reflected in many European paintings of Christ and is said to be the symbol of "the teacher is teaching". But this "gang banger" symbol is not about teaching. It runs across many religious sects from Christianity to Satanism and many government officials who are seen in such paintings hoisting their call signs as a symbol for the house of Wicca to which they belong.

During rituals such as the Roman Catholic Mass, "the sign" is required at certain points: the laity sign themselves at the beginning of the Eucharist, at the Gospel and at the final blessing; additionally, the celebrant makes "the sign" over the bread and wine before the Words of Institution (i.e. words of Christ). In the Tridentine Mass the priest signs the bread and wine many times.

The motion: The sign of the Cross is made by touching the hand sequentially to the forehead, sternum, and both shoulders, accompanied by the Trinitarian formula: at the forehead: *In the name of the Father*; at the stomach or heart: *and of the Son*; across the shoulders: *and of the Holy Spirit/Ghost*; and finally: You Must Say **Amen**. Amen and Amun are the same person.

Remember AMEN or **Amun-Ra** (for which it stands?) You remember reading how Christianity was about worshiping the Sun-god on Sunday and the tale of Mithra in Greek Mythology, the parody of Osiris of Egypt?

122

The name Mithra was adopted by the Greeks and Romans as *Mithras*, chief figure in the mystery religion of Mithraism. At first identified with the Sun-god Helios by the Greeks, the syncretism of Mithra-Helios was transformed into the figure Mithras during the 2nd century BC, probably at Pergamum. This new cult was taken to Rome around the 1st century BC and dispersed throughout the Roman Empire. Popular among the Roman military, Mithraism spread as far north as (and you should hold on to your hat for this one) the Hadrian's Wall and the Germanic Lines or Germany.

Mithra was born on December 25th, of a virgin mother, had 12 disciples, died on the cross, and was resurrected, according to

Persian myths dating back to 1200 BC. Mithra was also adopted by Greeks along with other attributes that were later given to the fictional Jesus introduced by those same Greeks.

Let's continue the exploration, take a journey back in time and look at just how many times this story was told while the names were changed to protect the innocent (or shall I say the guilty). You have Jesus the Christ. Now wait, let's do it like this:

Jesus Christ is the parody of Dionysus of Greece existing around 500 BC, part Krishna of India 900 BC, a little bit of Attis of Greece existing at 1200 BC, a tiny bit of Mithra of Persia 1200 BC, a sprinkle of Horus of Egypt 3000 BC, son of Osiris and Isis, and a bucket full of Yahushúa Mashiach.

Mithra is the parody of Krishna of India, Horus of Egypt, and attributes of his Father, Osiris the Sun-god.

Dionysus of Greece is the parody of Krishna of India, a sprinkle of Attis of Greece, Horus of Egypt, son of Osiris and Isis.

Krishna of India is the parody of Horus of Egypt, son of Osiris and Isis.

Jesus the Christ's birthday is celebrated on December 25th along with Attis, Mithra, Dionysus; all born of virgins, all purported to have been born on December 25th in their respective years.

These characters share many more things in common than just birthdays. The character Jesus stole many nicknames from earlier myths attributed to real and fictional characters such as these:

Dionisus is the King of Kings, Alpha and Omega, so is Jesus.

Mithra was considered the Truth, and the Light of the World, as is Jesus.

Horus, like Jesus, was the Lamb of God.

Now the Greco's will tell you it does not matter that we celebrate Jesus' birthday on December 25th, or Easter on the day that is in sync with the end of the equinox. We don't know when Jesus was born. It just so happens to be a date we chose. SATAN YOU ARE A LIAR.

Well, the solstice just happens to fall on the same day the three kings follow the star Sirus as it points toward the direction of the sun. Right... would the Greco's like to try to sell me the Brooklyn Bridge?

Hey, the studies of Franz Cumont were outstanding. Mithraism was revealed in a conclusive manner. *Texts and Illustrated Monuments Relating to the Mysteries of Mithra* was published in 1894-1900, with the first English translation in 1903. Cumont's hypothesis, as the author summarizes it in the first 32 pages of his book, was that the Roman religion was a development of a Zoroastrian *cult* of Mithra (which Cumont supposes is a development from an Indo-Iranian one of *mitra*); that through state sponsorship and syncretism was disseminated throughout the Near- and Middle East, ultimately being absorbed by the Greeks, and through them eventually by the Romans.

Cumont's theory was a hit in its day, particularly since it was addressed to a general, non-academic readership that was, at the time, fascinated by the Orient and its hitherto (relatively) uncharted culture. This was the age when great steps were being taken in Egyptology and Ideology, preceded as it was by Max Müller's "Sacred Books of the East" series, that for the first time demonstrated that civilization did not begin and end with Rome and Greece, or even with Assyria and Babylon, which until then were widely considered to be the cradle of humanity. Cumont's book was a product of its time, and influenced generations of academics such

124

that the effect of Cumont's theories of syncretism are felt even a century later.

You see, what we have here is called "Interpretatio graeca". **Interpretatio graeca** is a Latin term for the common tendency of ancient Greek writers to equate foreign divinities to members of their own pantheon. Herodotus, for example, refers to the ancient Egyptian gods Amon, Osiris and Ptah as "Zeus", "Dionysus" and "Hephaestus", respectively. Jesus is no different. Jesus is the interpretatio graeca for Yoshua the Messiah or Yahushúa Mashiach.

Now according to research, Yahushúa came to earth and fulfilled some prophecies of old and established new ones. Like those in many of the writings of the Old Testament, Yahushúa speaks through the deception of the New Testament. He spends time teaching and warning about the Greco's, while speaking in parables to elude obvious perception of the Greco's and you may find many of his true statements lodged within the text of Canon #85. It was important for the Catholic Church to include in the writings of the message that "the kingdom was at hand".

The **complete** writings of the Messiah have been omitted from the canonical received text of the Catholic Church. This includes the "hand-me-down" version of the Scriptures in the King James authorized edition, but clues nevertheless seep through its pages; the breadcrumbs of the Truth that were inserted into Canon #85, which we will be exploring in my upcoming book *Searching for NOD* will prove to be interesting reading.

Canon #85 is an astro-theological literary hybrid, which through the Interpretatio graeca in the old and New Testaments has led to this uncomfortably inconvenient truth: that Christianity (as we know it) is a twisted LIE. **You must study to show yourself approved to God, a workman who rightly divides the word of truth.**

But rejoice because the Truth from the first chapter was administered to you and the revelation of the Hellenization in chapter two along with the secret missions to gobble up the true Hebrews by the CIA and Israel has been retold to the masses.

The act of transference of characters and their attributes was a lazy attempt to misguide the masses from finding the Truth, though effective. But those of us that have the Spiritual DNA of the Lost Sheep still exist.

In no way have I shared any information to be unkind to you if you believe in Christianity. I thought it would be better if you knew about the Truth of Christianity. I know what it is to be sold out from one cover to the other cover of a Bible. I know what it is go to church, which included Sunday, Wednesday, a Bible study, and a discipline time all in a week. I know what it is to pray and read and pray and read and challenge my life to the way of the

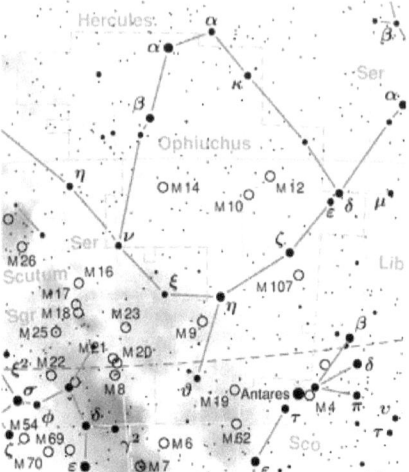

New Testament scriptures. I know what it is to be celibate for over ten years, hold my anger, repent, be patient, faithful, loving, humble, forgiving and confess ALL of my sins to a person. I know what it is like to tithe, give, serve, lead ministries, give hundreds and sometimes over one thousand dollars at one time to help the ministry. And that was during the years of my broke 20's. I know what it is to drop three or four people off after church, or feed an extra person for lunch after church. I know what it is to meet people at work, introduce them to Jesus, baptize them and assist them in their walks with God. I know how it hurts to watch someone do the same, then they decide to quit after doing this for five years or twenty-five years. For me this was True Christianity. I knew the Truth of Christianity, but let's just say I decided to listen and add to my learning. As stated earlier: I thought it would be better if you knew about the Truth of Christianity. Not my experience and not my truth, but the available, the researched, the hidden, The Revealed Truth! And this can only be found if we continue.

It's more important to know the TRUTH than to continue in the LIE. Yet, Christianity as a religious institution has been the biggest hoax played on mankind by the Greco's. Do you know that all of the

126

Wiccan Orders (Evil ones) have been waiting for this hour to bring about horror that you could not believe? They have been working toward the end of this age and preparing for the new age. Here- let me show you something. It's amazing how the obvious eludes people.

How many constellations do we have in the zodiac? 12, right? No, 13! That's right 13 constellations. It's kind of like the 13th floor on skyscrapers. It exists, but it doesn't exist. Hmmmmm......

Why is that? It lays on the celestial equator. The evil ones have known about this not just for years, but for ages.

Ophiuchus (Οφιούχος IPA: /ɒfiuck□s/) is one of the 88 constellations and was also one of the 48 listed by Ptolemy. Ophiuchus was formerly referred to as **Serpentarius** (/sɘp□ntɛ□ri□s/), the former originating in Greek and the latter in Latin, both meaning "serpent-holder". It is a large constellation located around the celestial equator between Aquila, Serpens and Hercules, northwest of the center of the Milky Way. The southern part lies between Scorpius to the west and Sagittarius to the east. Of the 13 zodiacal constellations (constellations that contain the Sun during the course of the year), Ophiuchus is the only one not counted as an astrological sign. Guess what happens when Ophiuchus and the Crux line up with the Sun. Well, it starts the clock all over again. It's what is called the end of an age and the beginning of a new age, which once again will take place at the end of year **2012**. It's represented by the alignment of the cross and the other celestial bodies in an ecliptic path--the symbol that is used by the Greco's to represent this is the **EIGHT ARM CROSS**. You have been looking at the gang signs of these clandestine cliques in everyday life, over and over again and there is a good chance you did not know what you where looking at. Here is a sample of an eight arm cross and the alignments along the celestial equator when the center of the Universe completes its rotation in the Great Year.

Check this out, Britain's Flag reflects the year were the Crux (cross) intersects with the other Heavenly bodies representing the end of the celestial Clock in 2012. The Confederate Flag shows the alignment of the 13th zodiac. The flag of Alabama reflects the alignment. The Flag of the State of Georgia includes Greek columns holding tympanum. The Flag of Vatican City reflects the two Keys crossing in the exact angle as the alignment and the Cross intersect at the cent. The Australian Flag reflects three symbols: the year of the eight armed cross and the Crux (Cross) and one big Star for which I don't know what it represent. New Zealand is the same and then there is the cross on the Grecian flag. Hmmmmm...What a web we weave.

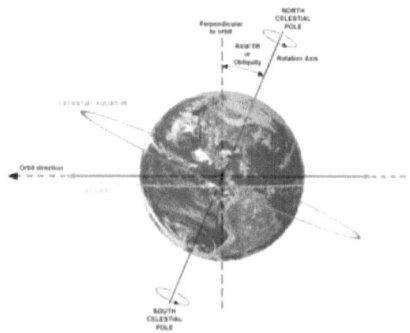

There are 13 stars in the Confederate Flag. Now what was that lie I was told when I was a kid about why there are 13 stars in many of the flags today, let alone 13 stripes? How about 13 feathers on the eagles of many of these countries' logos and letterheads? The fact of the matter is that the number 13 shows up constantly. Coincidence? I don't think so...

You see the **celestial equator** is a great circle on the imaginary celestial sphere, in the same plane as the Earth's equator. In other words, it is a projection of the terrestrial equator out into space. As a

128

result of the Earth's axial tilt, the celestial equator is inclined by ~23.5° with respect to the ecliptic plane.

An observer standing on the Earth's equator visualizes the celestial equator as a semicircle passing directly overhead through the zenith. As the observer moves north (or south), the celestial equator tilts

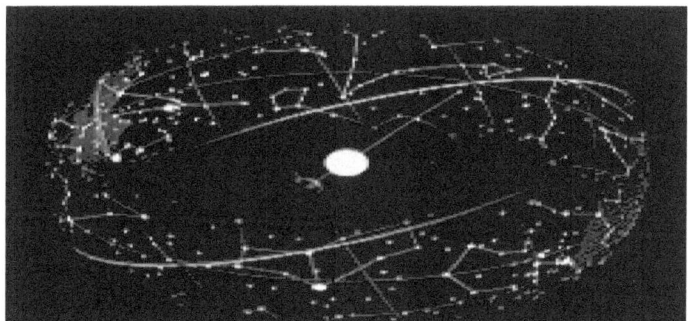

towards the southern (or northern) horizon. The celestial equator is defined to be infinitely distant (since it is on the celestial sphere); thus the observer always sees the ends of the semicircle disappear over the horizon exactly due east and due west, regardless of the observer's position on Earth. (At the poles, though, the celestial equator would be parallel to the horizon.)

Celestial objects near the celestial equator are visible worldwide, but they culminate the highest in the sky in the tropics. The celestial equator passes through these constellations:

You see, these Greco's know what's going down in December of 2012, but they are not telling the masses. We have over 80 flags and different state logos that reflect their anticipation for this upcoming event. How does this affect the Lost Sheep? I have not discovered that yet. But don't underestimate what is being written here.

You see, when God laid out the universe

he placed things in the exact place that were necessary for the ability to interpret time in PERFECT ORDER. Have you ever heard of GMT? You see that a lot in Movies, when individuals are doing search missions for a missing loved one, the search party marks their location by Greenwich Mean Time (GMT), which is a term originally referring to mean solar time at the Royal Observatory, Greenwich in London. It is now often used to refer to Coordinated Universal Time (UTC) when this is viewed as a time zone, although strictly UTC is an atomic time scale which only approximates GMT in the old sense. It is also used to refer to Universal Time (UT), which is the astronomical concept that directly replaced the original GMT. In the community of Greenwich, GMT (in the form of UTC) is the official time only during winter (during summer the time in Greenwich is British Summer Time rather than GMT).

Noon Greenwich Mean Time is not necessarily the moment when the Sun crosses the Greenwich meridian (and reaches its highest point in the sky in Greenwich) because of Earth's uneven speed in its elliptic orbit and its axial tilt. This event may be up to 16 minutes away from noon GMT (this discrepancy is known as the equation of time). The fictitious mean sun is the annual average of this nonuniform motion of the true Sun, necessitating the inclusion of *mean* in Greenwich Mean Time.

Historically the term GMT has been used with two different conventions for numbering hours. The old astronomical convention (before 1925) was to refer to noon as zero hours, whereas the civil convention during the same period was to refer to midnight as zero hours. The latter is modern astronomical and civil convention. The more specific terms UT and UTC do not share this ambiguity, always referring to midnight as zero hours.

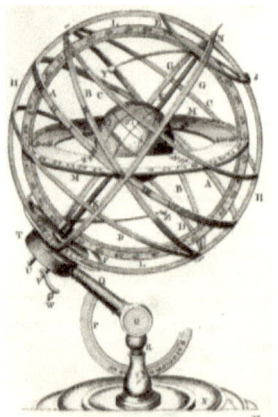

So why is this important? Well, remember the lie you were told that Christopher Columbus discovered America and that the Earth was considered flat before he made his voyage. Amazing..... Hey don't worry, I bought into that one myself, but these Greco's knew that the earth was not flat. They did not want the masses to know that they practiced alchemy and astrology, so they went to great lengths to misdirect the masses. Hey if you don't think so, then look at the picture below. It's an Armillary Sphere Machine. Armillaries pre-date the Christopher Columbus propaganda. These devices go way back to antiquity, back to the motherland in Egypt.

 Now according to recorded history the earliest known armillary sphere was invented by the ancient Greek Eratosthenes in 255 BC. The Chinese during the 1st century BC (Western Han Dynasty) also invented the armillary sphere, while the 2nd century Chinese astronomer Zhang Heng is credited as the world's first to apply motive power (using hydraulics) in rotating his armillary sphere. The name of this device comes ultimately from the Latin *armilla* (circle, bracelet), since it has a skeleton made of graduated metal circles linking the poles and representing the equator, the ecliptic, meridians and parallels (while the Chinese dubbed theirs as the *hun yi*, or *celestial-sphere instrument*). Usually a ball representing the Earth or, later, the Sun is placed in its center. It is used to demonstrate the motion of the stars around the Earth. Before the advent of the European telescope in the 17th century, the armillary sphere was the prime instrument of all astronomers in determining celestial positions.

Now how many times can one invention be invented? Was it invented in Greece or was it China? You see there are two very important balls in alchemy: one is a Chrystal ball the other is an Armillary sphere.

In its simplest form, consisting of a ring fixed in the plane of the equator, the *armilla* is one of the most ancient of astronomical instruments. Slightly developed, it was crossed by another ring fixed in the plane of the meridian. The first was an equinoctial, the second a solstitial armilla. Shadows were used as indices of the sun's positions, in combinations with angular divisions. When several rings or circles were combined representing the great circles of the heavens, the instrument became an armillary sphere.

So if the three kings was a true story, in Matthew chapter 2 when the Magi were summoned by King Herod to predict and prophecy about the birth of the new king, they would have used a portion of the Egyptian Mystery System to predict such events. They would have used a predated Armillary or use in conjunction with it. It's called an

Antikythera mechanism (shown to the right) which is an ancient mechanical calculator (also described as the first "mechanical computer") designed to calculate astronomical positions. It was discovered in the Antikythera wreck off the Greek island of Antikythera, between Kythera and Crete, in 1900. Subsequent investigation, particularly in 2006, dated it to about 150-100 BC, and hypothesized that it was on board a ship that sank en route from the Greek island of Rhodes to Rome.

You see, astrology and cosmology are not just reflected in the Wiccan's call signs and flags, but are also reflected in so called religious logos whether you are an Eastern Star or a worshiper of Satan, astrological coordinates are in their call signs and/or logos.

The **Order of the Eastern Star** is the largest fraternal organization in the world that both men and women can join. It was established in 1850 by Rob Morris, a lawyer and educator from Boston, Massachusetts who had been an official within the Freemasons. It is based on teachings from the Bible, but is open to people of all monotheistic faiths. It has approximately 10,000 chapters in twenty countries and

132

approximately one million members under its General Grand Chapter. Members of the Order are aged 18 and older; men must be Master Masons and women must have specific relationships with Masons. Their symbol has approximately the same coordinates along with the astrological circle as the satanic logo pictured.

Much more is available on this subject, but more importantly you must understand that the Catholic Church has limited power and all of the different houses including the Wicca clans that come from it, as well as the house that bears the Swastika, house of the Cross as worn on the robes of the KKK, the church under protest and so many more. All are limited in power.

You may notice that the astrological circle that is seen behind the head of Christ in many paintings is the same symbol as the order of the Eastern Star and the order of Sigil of Baphomet. Similarly, the hand sign of the Cross by the Catholic Church is similar to the Right hand of Baphomet gesture, the cross, which is the reference to their house of worship.

Pictured is a full picture of Baphomet (a symbol of satanic worship) as Baphomet shows the same hand sign the Catholic Church uses with the three fingers coming together referencing the trinity in the

left hand as it points down. The symbol at his waist is now used by modern medicine, but came from the Egyptian symbol Imhoptep which is the two snakes intertwined as they wrap around the tree of life or shall I say are representative DNA strands of the Serpent. This is a Representation of the Wicca Clan of the Serpents. On the top of Baphomet you will find the flaming torch between the horns which represents many of the Wicca religions such as Buddhism, Hinduism, and Jainism all worshiping the Dragon. In Buddhism they call the Dragon King Devadatta.

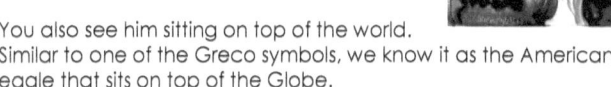

You also see him sitting on top of the world. Similar to one of the Greco symbols, we know it as the American eagle that sits on top of the Globe.

Now many in the modern day church will be quick to defend these signs and the astrological Circle of the Cross and attribute it to early

Christianity. It was generally rejected by the Reformers and is mostly absent from Protestantism and used as a sign only with the attempt to focus the masses on Jesus and to not focus on the origin of Jesus, the ones who created him and how they depicted him before he evolved into the Jesus character that we know today. They continued to draw and paint pictures of the fictional Jesus with a Bible in one hand and the Christian Sign in the other while reflecting the circle of the zodiac and the connection between the four stars that make up the Crux.

A system of **seven archangels** is an old tradition in **Abrahamic religions**. The earliest reference to a system of seven archangels appears to be in *Enoch I* (the Book of Enoch), where they are given as Michael, Gabriel, Raphael, Uriel, Raguel, Zerachiel and Remiel.

Centuries later, **Pseudo-Dionysius** gives them as Michael, Gabriel, Raphael, Uriel, Chamuel, Jophiel, and Zadkiel.

Pope Gregory I lists them as Michael, Gabriel, Raphael, Uriel, Simiel, Orifiel, and Zachariel.

Eastern Orthodoxy venerates Michael, Gabriel, Raphael, Uriel, Selaphiel, Jegudiel, and Barachiel.

Another Catholic variation lists them as follows, with corresponding days of the week: Michael (Sunday), Gabriel (Monday), Raphael (Tuesday), Uriel (Wednesday), Sealtiel (Thursday), Jhudiel (Friday) and Barachiel (Saturday).

In angelology, different sources disagree on the names and identities of the seven archangels. In the Book of Enoch, Remeil is also described as one of the leaders of the 200 Grigori, the fallen angels. Various occult systems associate each archangel with one of the traditional seven "luminaries" — the Sun, Moon, Mars, Mercury, Jupiter, Venus, and Saturn — but there is disagreement as to which archangel corresponds to which body.

The seven archangels figure in some systems of ritual magic, each archangel bearing a specific seal. This disclosure unlocks many of the so called mysteries of the book of Revelation. You see these symbols are clues. Follow the breadcrumbs people, follow the breadcrumbs.

In correspondence to the Angelic Seals and Celestial Maps of the seven seals you have **Musica universalis** (lit. **universal music**, or **music of the spheres**) which is an ancient philosophical concept that regards proportions in the movements of celestial bodies — the Sun, Moon, and planets — as a form of *musica* (the Medieval Latin name for music). This 'music' is not literally audible, but simply a harmonic and/or mathematical concept. The Greek mathematician and astronomer

Pythagoras is frequently credited with originating the concept, which stemmed from his semi-mystical, semi-mathematical philosophy and its associated system of numerology of Pythagoreanism. According to Johannes Kepler, the connection between geometry (and sacred geometry), cosmology, astrology, harmonics, and music is through *musica universalis*.

135

At that time, the Sun, Moon, and planets were thought to revolve around Earth in their proper spheres of orbit. The most thorough and imaginative description of the concept can be found in Dante's *Divine Comedy*. The spheres were thought to be related by the whole-number ratios of pure musical intervals, creating musical harmony. Johannes Kepler used the concept of the music of the spheres in his *Harmonice Mundi* in 1619, relating astrology (especially the astrological aspects) and harmonics.

There are three branches of the Medieval concept of musica:

> *musica universalis* (sometimes referred to as *musica mundana*)
>
> *musica humana* (the internal music of the human body)
>
> *musica instrumentalis* (sounds made by singers and instrumentalists)

In 2006, an experiment conducted by Greg Fox divided the orbital periods of the planets in half again and again until they were literally audible. The resultant piece was "Carmen of the Spheres". The principle of octaves in music states that whenever a sound-wave is doubled or halved in frequency, it yields another pitch similar in 'flavor' to the original one. This can be applied (through very large octave shifts) to any periodic cycle, including the orbits of celestial bodies.

Follow the bread crumbs people, follow the bread crumbs. The amount of energy that has gone into studying music and sound and how to unlock the sacred doors of geometry, similar to the tower of Babel, is extensive. These mysteries are available if you choose the right pill and take it. The Christian Church is riddled with astrology held hostage in Christian trappings, and the ministers and members of these churches sit and witness no power coming forth from a religion that promises power if you "believe". If two or more are gathered in his name and agree, then they shall receive whatever they desire if asked, and it shall be given. It's a LIE. If you don't think so, there have been over a billion Christians and not one of them, not even Benny Hinn, can state that every time two or more gather in Jesus' name that whatever they ask comes true. Keep reading.

It is about sound, the power is in the sounds. Archeologists, historians, and other people like myself search feverishly for information and clues on past societies and ancient ruins searching for clues, searching for the Land of NOD, "In the beginning was the word, and the word was with God, and the word was God." Remember that in the Book of John, or "In the Beginning God said let there be Light" in the book of Genesis. We have to recognize the Truth of sound and words, not this bankrupt language we speak, wasting our time, and how do people say it… Oh yeah, "waiting on the Lord". When you speak with the tongues of angels, whatever you speak to responds to your sound immediately, not this "wait on the Lord". I mean immediately.

Oh what was that? So where is it that I'm going with this? You may see and hear a lot of Christians and new age people talk about speaking to a situation. Some say based on the law of attraction if you think positive thoughts that you would have positive energy racing toward you, or if you say in the name of …. Then all things will be surrendered to you. But is it true, or are they parroting something they heard prior to studying facts?

Have you ever heard of the story of the Tower of Babel? It is in the Book of Genesis. Remember the book Moses was given credit for writing? Well, check this out. The symbols on the obelisks that the Pope and others confiscated contain dialect attributed to sacred geometry. It goes back to what is known as Pre-Babel. We live in a Post-Babel era. Here, let me give you more details.

Babel (Hebrew: בָּבֶל; *Bavel*) (Arabic: بابل; *Babel*) is the name used in the Hebrew Bible and the Qur'an for the city of **Babylon** (Akkadian **Babilu**), notable in Genesis as the location of the Tower of Babel.

In Gen. 11:9, the name of Babel is etymologized by association with the Hebrew verb *balal*, "to confuse or confound": *Balal* is regarded as a contraction of earlier *balbal*. The name *bab-ilu* in Akkadian means "gate of god" (from *bab* "gate" + *ilu* "god"). The word *bab-el* can also be seen to mean "gate of god" (from *bab* "gate" + *el* "god"). Remember "El" in Elohist, the "el" in angel, the "el" in Gabriel, Michael (and the other angels mentioned earlier)?

According to Genesis 11:1–9, humankind traveled after the flood from the mountain where the Ark rested, and settled in "a plain in the land of Shinar." Here, they attempted to build a city and a tower whose top would be in the Heavens, the Tower of Babel.

The attempt to build the city of Babel with its tower caused God to respond. He confused the language of the people, ultimately halting the project, and scattered them across the earth.

Well, what they were really building was a portal between this world and Heaven, not a physical "tower". **Bab** meant gateway and **El** meant God, hence, a "gateway to God". Come on now, don't you remember about bringing things to the altar, praying at the altar, or as some call it the pulpit. It's a representation of a doorway. A doorway! You bring animals and sacrifice them at the doorway, you get married at the doorway, and the preacher speaks to you standing in the doorway, while through divination he stands as "the voice of God". Oh yeah and many preachers would say "the Lord is telling me something, Yes, Lord, I'll tell them Lord." What do you think the ministers are doing while standing in the gateway? They are "channeling", and many times they are channeling unsuccessfully. Outside of promising to exchange blessing for tithes and offerings, they claim to be listening to the spirit of God and speaking as the voice of God.

You see, back in the day you would speak to anything and the thing you spoke to would respond to your speech because we spoke with tongues of Angels. It's like speaking in tongues as in Acts Chapter 2 with the understanding that tongue meant language and those tongues made things happen. Now in a post-Babel era, we speak with tongues of Men in a dead jumble dialect, bankrupt of its power, thanks to the Grimm Levites who are known for …

You see post-Babel grammar was not established for more effective communication. It was not a benevolent gesture, but a malevolent attempt at turning your phonetic structure upside down and striping the power in your words. The plagiarized story of the Tower of Babel represented that turning point.

So does it make sense now why your government continues to put an ancient dialect on its money and its state symbols? Latin… I don't think so. There is a reason for the "all-seeing eye" on the back of the dollar.

The race for enlightenment, the race for a higher conscience, for a more effective spiritual life are all fueled by the power of the tongue-the power of the spoken word. The power of the tongue is why archeologists, historians, and even I are digging through the dirt, surfing across waves of information, continuously searching for the "Rosetta Stone" that would decode the tongues of Angels.

Let me ask you a question about "the Fall of Man". What tree did he, or they eat from? What was that now, oh yeah, The Tree of THE KNOWLEDGE OF GOOD AND EVIL. The one tree they were forbidden to eat from. Say it with me now, "The Tree of **THE KNOWLEDGE OF GOOD AND EVIL**," and suddenly their eyes were opened. Now, what did God do about the Garden of Eden after that

event? That's right, he put Cherubim's, "Gatekeepers", east of the Garden of Eden to keep man out after driving him out, so that man would not eat of The Tree of Life and live forever in his new state of consciousness, which is defined "as one of us" according to God, according to Canon #85. Let's not forget he also added a flaming sword which turned every way to guard the way of the Tree of Life.

Why did he do that? Well, according to the Book of Genesis, if they were to eat of The Tree of Life after partaking of The Tree of THE KNOWLEDGE OF GOOD AND EVIL, God said that man has become as one of us, knowing both good and evil, if he puts forth his hand to eat from The Tree of Life he will live forever. Not only had Man become as one of "them", Man would also live forever, similar to God himself! So I must ask you, then, what is the tree of THE KNOWLEDGE OF GOOD AND EVIL and what did man possess for a short time that was so precious after eating from it? They experienced "something" from the time they ate to the time they were banished from the Garden. What did man posses that gave him dominion—so much dominion that they were sent away from the Garden? It's the same thing that Hitler, Stalin, Benjamin Franklin, The Grimm Brothers from Germany, the Pope, American , Israel, Persia, China, Europe governments, and all of the mights of this earth searched for or shall I say are searching for. NOD! The power in "words"; the power to manifest anything through "words". There has been a continuous Search for NOD.

Our modern day words and symbols are clues, bread crumbs to this answer. These words and symbols do exist, and here is the last bit. You witness the symbols of Satan, like President Bush signing to some fellow University Of Texas Long Horns Alumni. Many neopagans use this as a symbol of the horned god to identify each other; in this context it, is referred to as the "Sign of the Horned God". Some say that it is meant to ward off — or to bestow — the evil eye. It is also a representation of the Devil by some Satanists. The gesture's origin is believed to be an imitation of the shape of a goat's head, which has many associations with the concept of Satan in Christianity. Satan's Goat? Baphomet?

It has a variety of other meanings as well, depending on culture and area. In some places it is a sexual insult, charging a man with being a victim of cuckoldry (this insult is most common in Spain and Italy but is also used in Brazil). Perhaps because of its occult significance, it is used as a salute by fans of heavy metal music. If one reverses the extended fingers, one gets the "inverted heavy metal salute" which can be given as a reply to a heavy metal salute. In this case, the sign is known as "devil horns".

Do you see the sign being made in these pictures? To Chaotes practicing "Lovecraftian magick", it is called the "Sign of Voor" or the "Voorish Sign". Signs and symbols must be explored to get the full understanding of how Christianity is a mock version of Egyptian worship and religiosity. The Greco's have used these symbols to mimic the ancient and protected mystery teachings that have been (or at least attempted to be) incorporated into our daily lives. For example, let's take the **obelisks** that were a prominent part of the architecture of the ancient Egyptians, who had strategically placed them in pairs at the entrances of temples.

The **word, only the word** "obelisk" is of Greek rather than Egyptian origin because Herodotus, the **Greek** traveler, was the first to describe the objects to the European communities. Twenty-eight ancient Egyptian Obelisks are known to have survived, plus the "Unfinished Obelisk" found partly hewn from its quarry at Aswan. These obelisks are now dispersed worldwide for various reasons and circumstances with only eight remaining in Egypt.

The earliest temple obelisk still in its original position is the 68 ft. high red granite Obelisk of Senusret I of the XIIth Dynasty at Heliopolis.

The obelisk symbolized the sun-god Ra, or Re as some know him, and during the brief religious reformation of Akhenaton was said to be a petrified ray of the Aten, the sundisk. It was also thought that the god existed within the structure.

It is hypothesized by New York University Egyptologist Patricia Blackwell Gary and *Astronomy* senior editor Richard Talcott that the shapes of the ancient Egyptian pyramids and obelisks were derived from natural phenomena associated with the sun (the sun-god Ra also known as Osiris being the Egyptians' greatest deity). The pyramid and obelisk would have been inspired by previously overlooked astronomical phenomena connected with sunrise and sunset: the zodiacal light and Sun pillars, respectively.

The obelisk, called TEJEN in the sacred language of the ancient Egyptians, was a term which was synonymous with "protection" or "defense." The needle of stone had the function of perforating the clouds and dispersing negative forces that always threaten to accumulate, in the form of visible storms

or invisible ones, and was placed over the temple as a symbol of a petrified ray. The obelisk is composed of two parts: the body and the pyramid on. The body is a long block of a conic trunk section and the pyramiding symbolizes the rays of the sun. The top is the point of a pyramid formation which crowns the monolith and rested on a base. It was plated in gold, a metal which the Egyptians affirmed was the "flesh of the gods." The obelisks originated from the granite quarries of Aswan. In this place an unextracted obelisk still remains within the layer of rock. To 1.200 tons, it would have been the tallest, but was abandoned for the workman due to the appearance of fissures in the stone. It may have been the match for the Lateranense obelisk, a possible reason why there is only one in Karnak

The Romans were infatuated with obelisks and the power that they represented, to the extent that there are now more than twice as many obelisks standing in Rome as remain in Egypt. All fell after the

Roman period except for the Vatican Obelisk and were re-erected in different locations. The tallest Egyptian obelisk graces the square in front of the Lateran Basilica in Rome.

Not all the Egyptian obelisks re-erected in the Roman Empire were set up at Rome. Herod the Great imitated his Roman patrons and set up a red granite Egyptian

142

obelisk in the Hippodrome (racetrack) of his grand new city Caesarea in northern Judea. It was discovered by archaeologists and has been re-erected at its former site.

In Constantinople, the Eastern Emperor Theodosius shipped an obelisk in AD 390 and had it set up in his Hippodrome, on a specially-built base, where it has weathered Crusaders and Seljuk's and stands in the Hippodrome Square in modern Istanbul.

Rome is the "obelisk capital" of the world. The most prominent is the 25.5 m obelisk at Saint Peter's Square in Rome. The obelisk has stood since AD 37 on its site on the wall of the Circus of Nero, flanking St Peter's Basilica:

At the center of the ellipse stands an **Egyptian obelisk of red granite, 25.5 meters tall,** supported on bronze lions and surmounted by the Chigi arms in bronze; **in all, 41 meters to the cross on its top**. The obelisk from the 13th century BC was moved to Rome in AD 37 by the Emperor Caligula to stand in the central *spina* of the **Circus Gai et Neronis**, which lay to the left of the present basilica. It was moved to its current site in 1586 by the engineer-architect Domenico Fontana under the direction of Pope Sixtus V; the engineering feat of re-erecting its vast weight was memorialized in a suite of engravings (*illustrated right*). The Vatican Obelisk is the only obelisk in Rome that has not toppled since ancient Roman times. During the Middle Ages, the gilt ball on top of the obelisk was believed to have contained the ashes of Julius Caesar. Fontana later removed the ancient metal ball, (now in a museum in Rome) that stood atop the obelisk and found only dust. Though Bernini had no influence in the erection of the obelisk, he did use it as the centerpiece of his magnificent piazza.

These Greek organizations have stolen philosophies, religious rituals, religious artifacts, and even magical obelisks weighing tons. When you find 28 obelisks in Egypt that report having magical applications and then disburse the majority of them all over the world as symbols of dominance one would have to ask, why? Is their magic just folklore?

Why did **the Pope have this mega ton structure shipped over and placed in the center of the Circus Gai et Neronis and have a Cross Set on top**? Why do you find these symbols in Turkey shown on the previous page?

A number of obelisks were carved in the ancient Axumite Kingdom of Ethiopia. The most notable example – the 24 m high Obelisk of Axum carved around the 4th century AD – was looted by the Italians after the Second Italo-Abyssinian War and taken to Rome in 1937 where it stood in the Piazza di Porta Capena. Italy agreed in a 1947 UN agreement to return the obelisk, but didn't first truly affirm its agreement until 1997, after years of pressure. In 2003 the Italian government made the first steps toward its return, and as of 2006 it is in Axum still awaiting re-erection, attributed to the discovery of older burial chambers on the intended site.

Why is it in Ethiopia? The obelisk of Great Stele at Axum, now fallen, at 33 m high and 3 by 2 meters at its base is the largest single piece of stone ever worked in human history. It probably fell during erection or soon after, destroying a large part of the massive burial chamber underneath it. Why is there one in Caracas Venezuela and other places all over the world? Here is a list:

St Luke Old Street (church), Buckinghamshire, Tsarskoe Selo, Gatchina, St Petersburg, Stockholm, North Yorkshire, Villa Torlonia, Reggio Emilia, Anwoth Scotland, Wellington, Somerset, Springfield, Illinois, Kurnell, New South Wales, Bennington, Vermont, Montague, New Jersey, Foro Italico, Argentina, New Zealand, Dominican Republic, Barnaul, Victory Obelisk in Moscow, Ponce, Puerto Rico, North Dakota, Belo Horizonte, Brazil, Philippines, Arnaldo Pomodoro, Elizabethton, Tennessee, Buffalo, New York, Chalmette, Louisiana, and **many** other locations.

I must ask you, my assistant, with all truth and sincerety, Why? I beg of you to look at the picture below and go find out the answer to this question: **"What does this mean?"**

In Closure

The very word "secrecy" is repugnant in a free and open society; and we are as a people inherently and historically opposed to secret societies, to secret oaths and to secret proceedings. We decided long ago that the dangers of excessive and unwarranted concealment of pertinent facts far outweighed the dangers which are cited to justify it. Even today, there is little value in opposing the threat of a closed society by imitating its arbitrary restrictions. Even today there is little value in insuring the survival of our nation if our traditions do not survive with it. And there is very grave danger that an announced need for increased security will be seized upon by those anxious to expand its meaning to the very limits of official censorship and concealment that I do not intend to permit to the extent that it is in my control. And no official of my Administration, whether his rank is high or low, civilian or military, should interpret my words here tonight as an excuse to censor the news, to stifle dissent, to cover up our mistakes or to withhold from the press and the public the facts they deserve to know.

It requires a change in outlook, a change in tactics, a change in missions--by the government, by the people, by every businessman or labor leader, and by every newspaper. For we are opposed around the world by a monolithic and ruthless conspiracy that relies primarily on covert means for expanding its sphere of influence--on infiltration instead of invasion, on subversion instead of elections, on intimidation instead of free choice, on guerrillas by night instead of armies by day. It is a system which has conscripted vast human and material resources into the building of a tightly knit, highly efficient machine that combines military, diplomatic, intelligence, economic, scientific and political operations.

President John F. Kennedy
Waldorf-Astoria Hotel
New York City, April 27, 1961

He That Has an Ear, Let Him Hear!

OLD TESTAMENT Authors

Book	Catholic Church Attributed Authors	Many Scholars and Examinants Attributed Authors
Book of Genesis	Moses	Various authors from 9th century BC to last fifth century BC, including the Jahwist, Elohist, Deuteronomist and the Priestly sources[1]
Exodus		
Leviticus		
Numbers		
Deuteronomy		
Joshua	Joshua with a portion by Phinehas or Eleazar	Deuteronomist using material from the Yahwist and Elohist
Judges	Samuel	Deuteronomist
Ruth	Samuel	A later author, writing after the time of David
1 Samuel	Samuel, Gad, and Nathan	Deuteronomist or a combination of a Jerusalem source, republican source, the court history of David, the sanctuaries source, the monarchial source, and the
2 Samuel		

		material of various editors who combined these sources
1 Kings 2 Kings	Perhaps Ezra	Deuteronomist
1 Chronicles 2 Chronicles	Ezra	The Chronicler, writing between 450 and 435 BC, after the Babylonian captivity
Ezra	Ezra	The Chronicler, writing between 450 and 435 BC, after the Babylonian captivity
Nehemiah	Nehemiah using some material by Ezra	The Chronicler, writing between 450 and 435 BC, after the Babylonian captivity
Tobit		A writer in the second century BC
Judith	Eliakim (Joakim), the high priest of the story	
Esther	The Great Assembly using material from Mordecai	An unknown author writing between 460 and 331 BC
1 Maccabees	A devout Jew from the Holy Land.	An unknown Jewish author, writing around 100 BC
2 Maccabees	Based on the writing of Jason of Cyrene	An unknown author, writing in the second or first century BC

3 Maccabees		An Alexandrian Jew writing in Greek in the first century BC or first century AD
4 Maccabees	Josephus	An Alexandrian Jew writing in the first century BC or first century AD
Job	Moses	A writer in the 4th century BC.
Psalms	Mainly David and also Asaph, sons of Korah, Moses, Heman the Ezrahite, Ethan the Ezrahite and Solomon	Various authors recording oral tradition. Portions from 1000BC to 200BC.
Proverbs	Solomon, Agur son of Jakeh, Lemuel and other wise men	An editor compiling from various sources well after the time of Solomon
Ecclesiastes	Solomon	A Hebrew poet of the third or second centuries BC using the life of Solomon as a vista for the Hebrews' pursuit of Wisdom. An unknown author in Hellenistic period from two older oral sources (Eccl1:1-6:9 which claims to be Solomon, Eccl6:10-12:8 with the theme of non-knowing)
Song of Solomon	Solomon	
Wisdom	Solomon	An Alexandrian Jew writing during the Jewish Hellenistic

		period
Sirach	Jesus the son of Sirach of Jerusalem	
Isaiah	Isaiah	Three main authors and an extensive editing process. Is1-39 "Historical Isaiah" with multiple layers of editing. Is40-55 Exilic & Is56-66 post-exilic.
Jeremiah	Jeremiah	Baruch ben Neriah[2]
Lamentations	Jeremiah	Disputed and perhaps based on the older Mesopotamian genre of the "city lament", of which the Lament for Ur is among the oldest and best-known
Letter of Jeremiah	Jeremiah	A Hellenistic Jew living in Alexandria
Baruch	Baruch ben Neriah	An author writing during or shortly after the period of the Maccabees
Ezekiel	Ezekiel	Disputed, with varying degrees of attribution to Ezekiel
Daniel	Daniel	An editor in the fourth century to mid-second century BC
Hosea	Hosea	
Joel	Joel	

Amos	Amos	
Obadiah	Obadiah	
Jonah	Jonah	Possibly a post-exilic (after 530 BC) editor recording oral traditions passed down from the eighth century BC
Micah	Micah	The first three chapters by Micah and the remainder by a later writer
Nahum	Nahum	
Habakkuk	Habakkuk	
Zephaniah	Zephaniah	Disputed; possibly a writer after the time period indicated by the text
Haggai	Haggai	
Zechariah	Zechariah	Zechariah (chapters 1-8); the later remaining designated Deutero-Zechariah, were possibly written by disciples of Zechariah
Malachi	Malachi or Ezra	Possibly the author of Deutero-Zechariah

New Testament Authors

Book	Catholic Church Attributed Authors	Many Scholars and Examinants Attributed Authors
Matthew	Matthew the Evangelist	An author who borrowed from both Mark and a source called Q
Mark	Mark the Evangelist	Perhaps Mark (John Mark), follower of Peter.
Luke	Luke the Evangelist	Dr. Luke or an unknown author who borrowed from both Mark and a source called Q
John	John the Apostle or John the Evangelist	An unknown author with no direct connection to the historical Jesus Jn 21 finished after death of primary author by follower(s)
Acts	Luke the Evangelist	An unknown author who also wrote Luke, Dr. Luke]
Romans	Paul the Apostle	Paul the Apostle
1 Corinthians		
2 Corinthians		
Galatians		
Ephesians	Paul the Apostle	Paul the Apostle or edited dictations from Paul
Philippians	Paul the Apostle	Paul the Apostle

Colossians	Paul the Apostle	Disputed; perhaps Paul coauthoring with Timothy
1 Thessalonians	Paul the Apostle	Paul the Apostle
2 Thessalonians	Paul the Apostle	An associate or disciple after his death, representing what they believed was his message[3]
1 Timothy	Paul the Apostle	Perhaps someone associated with Paul, writing at a later date
2 Timothy	Paul the Apostle	Perhaps someone associated with Paul, writing after his death
Titus	Paul the Apostle	Perhaps someone associated with Paul, writing after his death
Philemon	Paul the Apostle	Paul the Apostle
Hebrews	Paul the Apostle or possibly Luke the Evangelist, Clement of Rome or Barnabas	An unknown author, but almost certainly not Paul[4]
James	James the Just	A writer in the late first or early second centuries, after the death of James the Just
1 Peter	Peter	An author, perhaps Silas, proficient with Greek writing

2 Peter	Peter	Certainly not Peter[5]
1 John	John the Evangelist	An unknown author with no direct connection to the historical Jesus Same as Gosple of John.
2 John	John the Evangelist	An unknown author with no direct connection to the historical Jesus Final Editor of Jn 21
3 John	John the Evangelist	An unknown author with no direct connection to the historical Jesus Final Editor of Jn 21
Jude	Jude the Apostle or Jude, brother of Jesus	A pseudonymous work written between the end of the first century and the first quarter of the 2nd century
Revelation of Christ to John	John the Apostle	Perhaps John of Patmos

Committees Assembled by King James in 1601

King James' instructions made it clear that he wanted the resulting translation to contain a minimum of controversial notes and apparatus, and that he wanted the Episcopal structure of the Established Church, and traditional beliefs about an ordained clergy to be reflected in the new translation.

First Westminster Company, translating from **Genesis to 2 Kings**:

Lancelot Andrewes, John Overall, Hadrian à Saravia, Richard Clarke, John Layfield, Robert Tighe, Francis Burleigh, Geoffrey King, Richard Thomson, William Bedwell;

First Cambridge Company, translated from **1 Chronicles to the Song of Solomon**:

Edward Lively, John Richardson, Lawrence Chaderton, Francis Dillingham, Roger Andrewes, Thomas Harrison, Robert Spaulding, Andrew Bing;

First Oxford Company, translated from **Isaiah to Malachi**:

John Harding, John Rainolds (or Reynolds), Thomas Holland, Richard Kilby, Miles Smith, Richard Brett, Daniel Fairclough;

Second Oxford Company, translated the **Gospels, Acts of the Apostles**, and the **Book of Revelation**:

Thomas Ravis, George Abbot, Richard Eedes, Giles Tomson, Sir Henry Savile, John Peryn, Ralph Ravens, John Harmar;

Second Westminster Company, translated the **Epistles**:

William Barlow, John Spencer, Roger Fenton, Ralph Hutchinson, William Dakins, Michael Rabbet, Thomas Sanderson;

Second Cambridge Company, translated the **Apocrypha**:

John Duport, William Branthwaite, Jeremiah Radcliffe, Samuel Ward, Andrew Downes, John Bois, John Ward, John Aglionby, Leonard Hutten, Thomas Bilson, Richard Bancroft.

In January 1609, a General Committee of Review met at Stationers' Hall, London to review the completed marked texts from each of the six companies. The committee included John Bois, Andrew Downes, John Harmar, and others known only by their initials, including "AL" (who may be Arthur Lake).

Catholic Holy Days

In the <u>Catholic Church</u>, **Holy Days of Obligation** or **Holidays of Obligation**, less commonly called **Feasts of Precept**, are the days on which, as <u>Canon 1247</u> of the Code of <u>Canon Law</u> states,

> *the faithful are obliged to participate in the <u>Mass</u>. Moreover they are to abstain from those works and affairs which hinder the worship to be rendered to God, the joy proper to the Lord's day, or the suitable relaxation of mind and body.*

Placed in the order of the civil calendar, the ten days (apart from Sundays) that this canon mentions are:

- <u>1 January</u>: <u>Solemnity of Mary, Mother of God</u>
- <u>6 January</u>: the <u>Epiphany</u>
- <u>19 March</u>: <u>Solemnity of St. Joseph, Husband of the Virgin Mary</u>
- Astrologic Calendar (Thursday of the sixth week of <u>Easter</u>) the <u>Ascension</u>
- Astrologic Calendar of Christ (Thursday after <u>Trinity Sunday</u>): the <u>Body and Blood</u>
- <u>29 June</u>: <u>Solemnity of Sts. Peter and Paul, Apostles</u>
- <u>15 August</u>: the <u>Assumption of the Blessed Virgin Mary</u>
- <u>1 November</u>: <u>All Saints</u>
- <u>8 December</u>: the <u>Feast of the Immaculate Conception</u>
- <u>25 December</u>: (<u>Christmas</u>) the Nativity of our Lord Jesus Christ

The Holy days or the days of worship by the Catholic Church correspond with the major events of astrology including the solar equinoxes like The Eucharist or Communion.

Reference Material

1. ^ "The Jewish Messiah: The Criteria." Jews for Judaism.
2. ^ Piper, John. "Christ Conceived by the Holy Spirit," *Desiring God*, 1984. Online: [http://www.desiringgod.org/ResourceLibrary/Sermons/ByDate/1984/429_Christ_Conceived_by_the_Holy_Spirit/ Resources from the ministry of John Piper. Accessed 09-26-2007
3. ^ Max Heindel, *The Rosicrucian Cosmo-Conception* (Part III, Chapter XV: Christ and His Mission), November 1909, ISBN 0–911274–34–0
4. ^ *Science and Health* 334
5. ^ Jewish Encyclopedia: Tarfon: "R. □arfon was extremely bitter against those Jews who had been converted to the new faith; and he swore that he would burn every book of theirs which should fall into his hands (Shab. 116a), his feeling being so intense that he had no scruples against destroying the Gospels, although the name of God occurred frequently in them."
6. ^ *The Canon Debate*, McDonald & Sanders editors, 2002, pages 414-415
7. ^ The Seventh Arian (or Second Sirmium) Confession Sirmium (357)
8. ^ Theodosian Code XVI.1.2 Medieval Sourcebook: Banning of Other Religions by Paul Halsall, June 1997, Fordham University, retrieved Septembe 25, 2006; IMPERATORIS THEODOSIANI CODEX Liber Decimus Sextus, Emperor Theodosius, George Mason University retrieved September 25, 2006; Theodosian Code XVI.1.2; Catholic Encyclopedia: Theodosius I: "In February, 380, he and Gratian published the famous edict that all their subjects should profess the faith of the Bishops of Rome and Alexandria (Cod. Theod., XVI, I, 2; Sozomen, VII, 4)."
9. ^ The Rosicrucian Fellowship: *The Rosicrucian Interpretation of Christianity*
10. ^ Albert Pike, *Morals and Dogma of the Ancient and Accepted Scottish Rite of Freemasonry, XXX: Knight Kadosh*, p. 822, 1872
11. *Ancient Egypt: The Light of the World* by Gerald Massey - online: http://www.theosophical.ca/AncientEgyptIntroduction.htm
12. web site dedicated to Gerald Massey
13. ^ Wenham, Gordon. "Pentateuchal Studies Today", Themelios 22.1 (October 1996)
14. ^ Gordon Wenham. "Exploring the Old Testament: Vol. 1, the Pentateuch," p160 (2003).
15. ^ For a brief overview of the Enlightenment struggle between scholarship and authority, see Richard Elliott Friedman, "Who Wrote the Bible?", pp.20-21 (hardback original 1987, paperback HarperCollins edition 1989).
16. ^ Gordon Wenham, "Exploring the Old Testament: Volume 1, the Pentateuch", (2003), PP.162-163.

17. ^ Don Closson (Probe Ministries), "Did Moses Write the Pentateuch?", and Richard Elliott Friedman, "Who Wrote the Bible?", pp.22-24.
18. ^ Richard Elliott Friedman, "Who Wrote the Bible?", p.25., and Alexander Rofe, "Introduction to the Composition of the Pentateuch", (1999), ch.2. See also Raymond F. Surberg, "Wellhausianism Evaluated After a Century of Influence", section II, *The Contribution of the Prolegomena from a Critical Viewpoint*.
19. ^ Richard Elliott Friedman, "The Bible with Sources Revealed", 2003; and Reading the Old Testament: Source Criticism.
20. ^ Richard Elliott Friedman, "Who Wrote the Bible?" esp. p.188 ff.
21. ^ Gordon Wenham, "Exploring the Old Testament", p.171.
22. ^ This is a highly schematised account of a complex argument: see Gordon Wenham, "Exploring the Old Testament", pp.167-171.
23. Meiri, Baruch 2001, "The Dream Behind Bars: The Story of the Prisoners of Zion from Ethiopia", Gefen Publishing House. ISBN 965-229-221-4
24. Poskanzer, Alisa 2000, "Ethiopian Exodus", Gefen Publishing House. ISBN 965-229-217-6
25. Rosen, Ricki 2006, "Transformations: From Ethiopia to Israel", Gefen Publishing House. ISBN 965-229-377-6
26. Samuel, Naomi 1999, "The Moon is Bread", Gefen Publishing House. ISBN 965-229-212-5
27. Shimron, Gad 2007, "Mossad Exodus; The Daring Undercover Rescue of the Lost Jewish Tribe", Gefen Publishing House. ISBN 978-9652294036
28. Yilma, Shmuel 1996, "From Falasha to Freedom: An Ethiopian Jew's Journey to Jerusalem", Gefen Publishing House. ISBN 965-229-169-2
29. Holy Bible (Nelsons Regency Bible from Thomas Nelson Publishers){King James Version}
30. ^ "Theodosius I", The Catholic Encyclopedia, 1912.[1]
31. ^ "Man, Myth and Magic", Osiris, Vol 5 p2086, S.G.F Brandon, BPC Publishing, 1971.
32. ^ "Isis and Osiris", Plutarch, translated by Frank Cole Babbitt, 1936, Vol 5 Loeb Classical Library.[2]
33. ^ "The Historical Library of Diodorus Siculus", Vol 1, translated by G. Booth, 1814.[3]
34. ^ "Man, Myth and Magic", Osiris, Vol 5 p2087-88, S.G.F Brandon, BPC Publishing, 1971.
35. ^ "Osiris, Asar" retrieved 25 May 2005.[4]
36. ^ "Osiris", Man, Myth and Magic, S.G.F Brandon, Vol5 P2088, BPC Publishing.
37. ^ "The Historical Library of Diodorus Siculus", translated by George Booth 1814. retrieved 03 June 2007.[5]
38. ^ Plutarch. "Section 13", *Isis and Osiris*, 356C-D. Retrieved on 2007-01-21.

39. De Santis, Marc G. "At The Crossroads of Conquest." *Military Heritage*, December 2001. Volume 3, No. 3: 46–55, 97 (Alexander the Great, his military, his strategy at the Battle of Gaugamela and his defeat of Darius making Alexander the King of Kings).

40. Fuller, J.F. C; *A Military History of the Western World: From the earliest times to the Battle of Lepanto*; New York: Da Capo Press, Inc., 1987 and 1988. ISBN 0-306-80304-6

41. Gergel, Tania Editor *Alexander the Great* (2004) published by the Penguin Group, London ISBN 0-14-200140-6 Brief collection of ancient accounts translated into English

42. Blueletter.org

43. Wikipedia.org

44. American Heritage Encyclopedia

45. http://egipto.com/obeliscos/histo2.html

SPECIAL THANKS FROM DE VON TO...

My father and mother, Larry and Emogene Bell. You have always been a father that cared, an initiate in search of truth, a 1961 Civil Rights Freedom Rider, entrepreneur, leader and brilliant individual who made it easy to be one of his boys. I have enjoyed being your son. My Mom has been a devoted Christian and teacher, a loving nurturing person that has shared her views on religion and started her sons on their paths to have relationships with God.

My wives, Candice Michelle and Kellie Marie Bell. Candice for your unwavering support . Kellie (RIP) for your intense love for God and continued studies with me on canon #85.

My brilliant daughters, Diamond, Ebonea, and Britney for reviewing this book over and over again while giving your comments and suggestions.

My co-author, Tiffany Duvernay, for your tireless research, editing, contributions, and phenomenal knowledge of text in canon #85.

Tom and Karen Driscoll for your hospitality while journeying to Washington DC.; Karen for editing, providing suggestions and insight, and for sharing your knowledge of history and Egyptian culture.

Dion Gordon, my brother in the Lord; I salute you **"For the Kingdom"**.

SPECIAL THANKS FROM TIFFANY TO...

My grandmother, Inez C. Taylor (RIP) and my mother, Phyllis I. Duvernay (RIP). Granma for being my biggest cheerleader and for your undying love for me. Mommy for giving me the world, taking me around the world, instilling morals and loving me. Thank you both for your example of devotion to God and teaching me the love and tenacity required to complete this research.

My father, Leonard Duvernay Jr., for your love, compassion, knowledge, intellect, wit and amazing sense of humor. Once best friends, always best friends!

My aunt, Karen Driscoll. Auntie Karen thank you so much for inhabiting the love of my mom and grandmother. I never thought we would work on such a project together. Your awareness, knowledge, intuitiveness and love are off the register!

My co-author, De Von Bell, for your endless passion, all night research, tenacity, knowledge and willingness to learn. We fought hard for this!

*Our Family and friends that helped us research canon #85 and subject matters that lead to the works of this book including, but not limited to, my brothers, D'Andre and Le Shaun E. Bell (RIP), Pat Loveless, Gina Marcello, Michelle Breaux, Orlando Love, Bishop Howard Swancey, Michelle Latson, Michele and La Teef Moses, Charletta "Chachie" Royster, Valerie Parham, Merlie Huey, Barbara Talalemotu, Fabian Williams, Tim Blake and Ernesto Villegas.

Lastly, we thank God for our individual journeys, our journey together, and guiding us to so much syncretistic information throughout the years. It all came together for such a time as this.

Be sure to read other books by Quantum Door Publishing, Inc.:
Which Way Does Power Flow?
Searching for NOD!
RED LETTER

WWW.QDEXPERIENCE.COM

Thank you for your assistance. You are free to go!

www.ingramcontent.com/pod-product-compliance
Lightning Source LLC
Chambersburg PA
CBHW030530020726
47494CB00004B/1301